Also by Ann Nolan Clark

Summer Is for Growing

Ann Nolan Clark
Illustrated by Agnes Tait

Farrar, Straus & Giroux

New York **A Bell Book**

Copyright © 1968 by Ann Nolan Clark
Library of Congress catalog card number: 68–13684
First printing, 1968
All rights reserved

Printed in the United States of America
by Mahony & Roese
Designed by Berry Eitel

Published simultaneously in Canada by
Ambassador Books, Ltd., Rexdale, Ontario

*To some little girls I knew who now
are Big Girls.*

Marie Nolan
Kathleen and Aileen Wheeler
Jeffner and Vanann Allen
Linda and Brenda Nolan

Contents

Summer Is for Growing

SUMMER IS FOR GROWING *is the story of the haciendas of New Mexico in the year 1851.*

Over the Palace of the Governors in Santa Fe, the Spanish flag had flown, and then the flag of Mexico. In 1850, New Mexico had become a territory of the United States of America. The flag of the United States replaced the flag of Mexico over the Palace of the Governors.

The Spanish Conquistadors and their descendants had been loyal subjects of the King of Spain in the New World land of New Spain. When Mexico replaced Spain in government, most of the descendants of the early Spanish explorers and conquerors felt neglected and dissatisfied. Now that the flag of the United States of America was flying over the seat of government in Santa Fe, most of the Spanish thought they were pleased, but they were not certain.

Each person for himself had to understand what the new flag stood for and then what would be his devotion, his loyalty, and his responsibility to the Stars and Stripes of the Union.

This is the story of a young girl of this time and how she accepted what she thought was her responsibility and kept what she thought had been her promise.

Time: June, July, and into August, 1851

Place: A mythical hacienda—but there were many like it—between Rancho de Taos on the edge of the great Indian Pueblo Taos, and Mora, a French-Spanish town made up mostly of Hudson's Bay Company trappers.

 *Chapter One*

Hacienda Sunrise

Lala was awake, but she did not open her eyes, did not move, lay quietly waiting—waiting for something. The large, high-ceilinged room was filled with the half-light of before dawn.

Faintly, the girl heard a rooster crowing. This would mean that sun was peeping over the hills of the Sangre de Cristo at the edge of the pasture. Between the pasture and the foothills flowed the river that fed the mother ditch and all the little feeder ditches that brought water to the hacienda, the orchard, the vineyard, and the milpa. At one side of the pasture were the high adobe walls enclosing the night corral for the horses.

At the thought of the corral and the horses there, Lala stirred, tensed, then lay quiet again. Each small happening of the morning came at its own time, in its own place. Lala knew this, knew she could not change the pattern of what was happening and what would happen next. She waited.

At last the big iron key turned heavily in its lock, the carved door on its heavy iron hinges swung inward slowly. The patio window shutters were opened and fastened against the thick adobe walls outside. Sunlight streamed in to fill the shadowed corners of the white-walled room.

Lala felt warm sunlight on her face, smelled earth and water and the scent of flowers. She opened her eyes so she could see as well as hear and feel and smell while she lay waiting. It was always this way. Each morning she waited to welcome with delight all the adventures the new day would bring. Her worry at night, before she closed her eyes to sleep, was what if she should forget to waken when tomorrow's morning came! But she never forgot. Always she was waiting for the grating key to turn, the creaking door to swing, and the soft sound the shutters made as they were pushed against the outside wall.

There were other sounds that greeted each day's coming. Blanca, the white cat, always leaped up upon the deep-set windowsill, arching her back and purring her morning invitation to the girl in the bed to be up and about, doing the things that she should do. The parrot in the patio outside the opened windows screeched a noisy greeting to all the other parrots in all the other patios of the hacienda and was screeched at in return.

Tranquilino's bare feet made little half sounds as he pattered across the patio to turn on the water in the fountain. He did not turn the water on and leave it, but kept turning it on full-force and half-force and dribble, testing it to get the right flow of water that he wanted. There must be enough flow to make a tinkle of music and a ribbon of silver, but not too much. Never too much. Water must be used sparingly and wisely and never wasted. Tranquilino understood this and was patient and slow in getting the exact and right amount that he thought was needed.

Added to the fountain water tinkle were the flat slaps of water being thrown by the handfuls from a wooden bucket upon the patio tiles. This was followed by the swish-swish of a handmade broom as

Carmen swept the dust she had dampened into small, neat piles. As she scooped out water and swept up dust, she scolded Tranquilino for being so slow in turning on the fountain. Slap—swish-swish—scold, slap—swish-swish—scold. It made a kind of song to accompany Pedro's whistling. Pedro whistled merrily as he sprinkled water on the patio flowers, and on Carmen and Tranquilino when he dared. Water was to be sprinkled, splashed, poured, thrown, thought the whistling Pedro, dodging Carmen's broom.

The small copper bell above the chapel door began to ring, a thin, clear sound. This was Rafael's work to ring the small bell at sunrise and again at sunset. But not the big bell hanging above the small one. The big bell was rung only for fiestas or as warning for an Indian raid. Luis the major-domo rang the big bell. Never Rafael.

Lala sat up in the high carved bed. How good it was, she thought, that each special sound belonged to the special person making it. It was good too, to know that each sound came from its special place and in its special time. Each morning was the same. The workers and the sounds they made came in order. The order never changed. The next sound would be made by Pita. It was.

10

The door swung wide. Pita came hurrying in with an armload of cedarwood for the corner fireplace fire. Pita was about Lala's age, although taller, thinner, darker. In their ways they were much alike: one, a French-Spanish girl in the high carved bed, and the other a Mexican-Indian lighting the fire.

When the dry wood sparked into flame, Pita rose and said primly, as she had been taught to say, "God give you a good day." Lala nodded an acceptance, but did not answer. This too, had been taught to her, as right and proper. Greetings over, the two small girls smiled at each other. Each one's smile promised the other that this day would delight them as all their days delighted them.

Nana came to the door. As swiftly flashing as her smile had been, Pita's bare brown feet were swifter, taking her from the room graceful as a young fawn in a mountain meadow.

Nana brought chocolate in a beautiful paper-thin porcelain cup that had come from Spain. "God give you a good day," she said, handing the cup to the girl sitting up in her bed.

Nana had been with Lala's mother and her Tante Rita almost all their lives. As a young woman, she had been brought from Mexico to take care of those two little French girls who had newly come to Taos

11

from New Orleans. Nana had taken care of them, played with them, scolded them when it had been necessary, and loved them for more than twenty years. They had never been separated. When the girls had been sent back to New Orleans for schooling, their parents had sent Nana with them. It was fortunate that the two girls had married brothers, Spanish men, they were, whose family had title to a vast land grant given them by the King of Spain. When the girls married and left the home of their parents in Taos, they went to the hacienda of their husbands' family. Nana went with them.

Nana was teaching her daughter Pita to take care of, play with, keep out of mischief when she could, and love the Patrona's daughter, Lala. Nana was as strict and firm with Lala as she was with Pita. Now she said, "Drink up. Do not dream over your cup of chocolate. Hurry. Hurry. Do not keep your mama, the Patrona, waiting."

Lala had no intention of dreaming over her chocolate. She intended to gulp the thick frothy drink as soon as Nana's back was turned.

Nana looked around the room, surveying it, seeing if everything was in order. "That Carmen," she mumbled. "Always making a great to-do with throwing water on the patio tiles and whisking her broom and scolding Tranquilino. She only half cleans if she is not watched." With pride she added, "But I watch," running her fingers over the straw-decorated dowry chest of the little señorita. No dust. No dust on the windowsill, where Blanca now was sleeping. She felt the paper flowers in the nicho that held the wooden statue of Saint Anne. They felt crisp and freshly made. No reason to scold Carmen. What a shame!

The parrot hopped in through the window opening. Nana was enraged. She shouted in fury: "Out. Out. Dirty one. Go with Carmen."

The cat stretched itself in cat content. Lala, seeing Nana was not looking, stuck out her tongue and licked the sweet froth from her lips, her eyes sparkling with mischief. The Indian woman opened the double doors of the ceiling-high, hand-carved walnut armoire that held the little Lala's clothes. Ah, there would be discussion, she thought with pleasant anticipation, and she, Nana, would be victorious.

Lala stood behind her. "With your permission, Nana, the white chemise with the blue embroidered flowers and my indigo dyed skirt from Mexico."

"The white chemise with the red embroidered flowers and the red flannel skirt," Nana ordered.

Lala tried again: "With your permission, Nana,

today I will wear my cloth slippers, the ones embroidered with gold thread."

Nana was shocked. "Leather sandals," she said. "This is not a feast day."

"I want my hair plaited in two braids like Pita's, and wound with yarn." Lala spoke firmly, watching Nana.

Sounds like her father, the patron, Nana thought, tying the black curls in back with a red-ribbon bow. Aloud she said, "And the red sash and the dark blue reboza, and into your mama's room at once. The Patrona must not be kept waiting."

Lala shrugged. She had known she could not wear fiesta clothes on an ordinary, working day. It was a kind of game she played with Nana. She smiled at the Indian woman and danced out into the patio, along the wide *portal,* and into her mother's room. As she danced, she sang:

> "*Tra-la-lala-la*
> *Tra-la-lala-la*
> *Tra-la-lala-la*
> *Tra-la.*"

Her mother's room was even larger than her own: high-ceilinged, with massive, hand-carved vigas and

14

hand-carved doors and thick adobe walls. The windows, as in Lala's room, had shutters instead of panes of glass. On the walls were hung painted tin-framed mirrors and hand-dipped candles in shining copper sconces. In the nicho in the fireplace chimney, wreathed in paper flowers, was a wooden statue of San Juan Bautista, and above the door a silver crucifix. The floor was of hardened earth, hand-polished, and covered with hand-woven brown and white blankets.

There were two armoires and many chests, some carved, some painted, some brassbound and studded, and others with straw design. The chest Lala liked best was paneled in mother-of-pearl and had many little drawers. One drawer, always partly opened, was filled with coins, Spanish, Mexican, American, of gold and silver. Lala stopped dancing long enough to dip her hands deep into the coin-filled drawer. Then she danced over to her mother's bedside.

This bed was very large, almost square, built of a solid mound of adobe, and padded with buffalo skins. The sheets were of hand-spun linen richly embroidered, and the colcha a soft wool covering stitched in yarn.

"Good morning, Maman." Lala spoke in French. Almost always she spoke French with her mother, in

Spanish always with the hacienda workers, and with her father in a mixture of French and Spanish. Now and then she tried a little English.

Maman smiled at her daughter. "You were dancing the varsovienne," she said, and she sang the words in Spanish:

> *"Put your little foot,*
> *Put your little foot,*
> *Put your little foot*
> *down here."*

"But I am singing it in English," Lala answered.

> *"Will the little foal,*
> *Will the little foal,*
> *Will the little foal*
> *be mine?"*

She knew that her mother understood English, although she would not speak it. She would understand the English words. Perhaps she would answer. It would be so easy for her mother, also, to make a song in English. She could sing:

> *"Yes, the little foal,*
> *Yes, the little foal,*
> *Yes, the little foal*
> *is yours."*

17

But she was disappointed. Her mother only laughed, singing again the Spanish words.

Lala touched her mother's hand. "But will the little foal be mine, Maman? Will Papa give it to me?"

Her mother shrugged. "How can I know? Receive my morning blessing, little daughter. You must not keep your father waiting."

Lala's eyes filled with tears. "But I need the foal. I need a good horse. That pinto I ride is a baby's pony, not a mount for one who is soon to begin her eleventh year."

Her mother did not answer, so Lala continued talking. "I want my own horse. My brother Baptiste has his horse. He had it long before Tío Toto took him to the States to school. My cousins Ricardo and Roberto have their horses. Why can I not own a horse? Why must I ride a pinto pony?"

"Annette," Maman spoke sharply. That she had used the baptismal name Annette, rather than the pet name Lala, meant that she was not pleased.

Quickly the girl wiped her eyes and knelt for her mother's morning blessing. Then she smiled at Maman, letting her smile say she was sorry. Her mother's returning smile said that her daughter was forgiven.

 *Chapter
Two*

*Into the Bright
Blue Morning*

Out in the patio, gaiety took possession of Lala's heart again. Pita was waiting for her, sitting patiently on the floor of the *portal.* Her dark blue rebozo, covering her long black braids, her head, and part of her face, had one end thrown over her shoulder, not because the morning was cool, but because this was the way a rebozo should be worn.

Lala stopped to touch her lightly, smiling down into the brown, oval face. Since Baptiste and the cousins had been taken to the States, the young

19

Mexican-Indian girl had been her only companion, and she loved and cherished her. Taking the girl's hand, Lala laughingly pulled her to her feet and began to sing. Pita, quick to follow every mood, joined in.

> *"Adios, mi chaparrita,*
> *No llores por tu Pablo.*
>
> *Ay! que caray. Ay! que caray."*

There were no dancing steps for this song, but it had a galloping melody. Both girls, still singing, galloped through the patio arch and out into the high-roofed, cobblestoned zaguán.

> *"Ay! que caray. Ay! que caray."*

The zaguán was wide, wide enough for a span of mules and a coach to enter. When the family went visiting or relatives came to visit, they were driven into the zaguán and stopped by the door of the sala. Into the zaguán came pack burros laden with trade wares from Mexico or wood for María's kitchen fire or sacks of wheat flour from the Patrón's mill. Men on horseback rode into the zaguán, also, when they came calling. It ran the length of the hacienda, dividing it, yet holding it together because through its length coursed the life activities of its people.

At one end, near the sala, which was opposite the kitchen, were giant double doors opening out into the courtyard of the Patrón's trading post. The heavy, high, wide doors were carved in panels of different sizes, and the heavy knocker was high enough for a man on horseback to use, announcing his arrival to the people inside the thick adobe walls. In a lower panel was a small door for one who walked to enter. This small door had its key left in its lock, but beside the double doors hung a foot-long iron key that fitted the square padlock for locking and unlocking. The great doors were unlocked only to let someone enter, and they were immediately locked again. Hidden in the carving of a panel was a peephole through which one could see who was pounding on the outside, friend or foe. Enemy Indian bands roamed the land, raiding, burning, killing. The people inside the hacienda walls were aware of this danger, lived with it and sang as they worked.

The zaguán, although it was actually a covered roadway, was wide and cool and beautiful. Like the rooms of the hacienda, the walls of the zaguán were whitewashed. Long ladders of colored corn and strings of scarlet chili peppers hung in gay festoons against the gleaming whiteness of the walls, where there were also nichos holding wooden saints and candle sconces made of painted tin.

Along the two sides of the zaguán were wide, low archways opening into *portal*-shaded, flower-bordered patios. By each archway was a parrot perch and a tall clay olla of water with its hanging gourd dipper to quench the thirst of all who passed by.

Men and women hurried to and fro, laughing, scolding, talking, singing, bringing wood and water, and sweeping, always sweeping.

María, singing in the kitchen as she cooked stacks of blue corn tortillas for the morning breakfast, called out to Lala as she passed: "Señorita, here are two tortillas, hot ones, made just for you." But the two girls did not hear her. They were too busy singing and galloping down the long zaguán.

Four young women hurried by. On their heads they carried piles of folded woolen winter blankets. They were taking them to the river to soak them in yuca suds, to pound them clean with rocks. Then the women would wade waist-deep in the wide, clear river, rinse the blankets, and lay them to dry on the grassy riverbank in the warm June sun.

22

Lala stopped to watch the women as they scurried along. She wished she were going with them. Last year when Tante Rita lived here they had taken the burro-drawn carreta down to the river to bring the women their noontime dinner. Maman had driven the little burro and Maman and Tante had sung all the way to the river and all the way back again. But that was last year. This year Maman had too much to do to go singing to the river. Lala sighed, but quickly she remembered where they were going. She began to clap her hands to the little running steps of the varsovienne.

The girls had reached the far end of the zaguán and the great doors leading into the patio with the blacksmith forge and enormous bullhide bellows. This was where the horses and mules were shod and the coach wheels mended. At its far end was the wagon shed, where the coach and carts were kept.

'Chacho was waiting for them by the wagon shed. 'Chacho, an orphan abandoned on the road from Mexico, had been taken to the hacienda and cared for there. Later the Patrón had trained him to be Lala's chore boy, taking care of the pinto that she rode and also taking care of Lala when she was outside the safety of the hacienda walls. Except for his morning "God bless your day," he seldom spoke to her, but when she was in his charge he was always near her, always watching over her, sometimes disapprovingly. Lala often did little things to tease him, for the mischief of watching his black look of disapproval, but more often she did little things to please him, bringing him small gifts for the delight in seeing his sad, serious face light up with joy.

The three children, now in single file, hurried through the gate in the wagon shed. On the other side of the high adobe wall, fenced in upright cedar posts, was the night corral, where the blooded horses were kept for safety.

"Ay! ay!" Lala whispered to Pita. "There they are, the dam and foal. Nothing has happened to them."

Then she saw the Patrón standing near the penned place where the dam and her foal were being kept. "Papá, papá," Lala called, joy in her voice at seeing him. He was her idol. She was his heart.

Almost at once, Lala remembered her manners. This was her father she was calling to, Patrón of the hacienda. Both as father and as Patrón he must be respected and revered. Affection must be cloaked in the formality of politeness. This had been taught her.

The little girl slowed her steps. Pita, behind her,

also slowed down, and 'Chacho continued to walk sedately at a discreet distance.

Lala looked at her father with pleasure. He stood so straight, so proud, so courteous, waiting her arrival as if she were the greatest lady of the land. He held his flat black hat in his hand by its chin strap. Behind him stood his favorite horse, El Dorado, golden horse of Spain, its heavy white mane like snow hand-spun in silken threads of white, its long white tail sweeping the ground. They made such a picture, Spanish gentleman and horse of gold, a picture to be looked at with love and remembered with tenderness.

The girl received her father's morning blessing, gave him the expected formal greeting in return. Then flashing her sunny smile, she turned her gaze to dam and foal in their pen in the corner of the corral. The long-legged foal, like its mother, was a rich creamy white with large oval spots as big as saucers dotting its body. The spots, perfect in shape, looked as if they had been embroidered with thick black yarn. Each small hoof was marked alike in stripes of black and white. Such a perfect body! Such a proud head! Such clear, intelligent eyes. Lala felt as if she could not breathe, beholding such beauty, such perfection.

She looked at her father again. Then at Luis, his major-domo, standing beside him, holding the horses. She acknowledged graciously Luis's morning greeting. Then taking a longer look, she recognized the horse he would ride, El Barb, her brother's horse.

Luis is riding El Barb, Baptiste's horse, she thought furiously. Why can I not ride El Barb? I am the one who should ride him when my brother is not here.

Her father, reading her thoughts, was amused. Pleased too, perhaps. The girl has no fear, he thought. Born to the saddle. What a proud, beautiful rider she will become in a few more years. A true Spaniard!

But he did not voice his pleasure. Aloud, he said, "As you see, Luis will ride El Barb this morning." Then he added, by way of explanation: "The Barb is a man's horse. A man must ride him to exercise now that your brother has been taken to the States."

Lala flushed. She could ride El Barb. She knew she could ride him if she had the chance. She would ride him, too, some day! But she knew she would not. She would never have the opportunity. There would always be 'Chacho. Pita would not tell, but 'Chacho would. 'Chacho would disapprove and he would tell.

She shrugged her shoulders.

French, like her mama, her father thought. Her

26

anger, quick to come, was as quick to leave. Like the flash of a silver trout in a river pool, her father thought, as the young girl turned again to watch the dam and her foal.

The Patrón beckoned a vaquero to take the foal from its dam and put it in a smaller pen. He said to his daughter, "The foal is now eight weeks old. It is time it begins to learn to trust man, its master." Then he added quickly, "Have no fear, Lalita. The dam can see its foal and know that all is well with it."

Touching his daughter's shoulder lightly, he directed her inside the pen, saying as he did so, "Walk slowly—slowly—slowly. Walk quietly. Even let your heart be quiet. Now touch it gently—gently. Touch it lightly. The foal must learn to trust you, little daughter."

This first meeting of foal and girl was for a moment only. Outside the pen again, Lala leaned against the cedar posts that made its wall. Her fingertips still could feel the quivering little body as she had touched it.

A dog barked sharply. It was the sheepherders' dog, helping to herd the flocks from the night corral to graze on the tufted grass of the rolling foothills. They walked in a dust cloud of their own making, digging their sharp hoofs into the sandy soil. Lala watched them, without knowing that she watched them, thousands of sheep herded along by their shepherds and the dog.

When the girl could speak, she asked her father shakily, "Am I to ride it then when it is old enough to have been broken?"

Her father looked at her, knowing that he must make a decision. Should he give her this foal, or dare he wait until August when perhaps—perhaps a palomino might be foaled?

 *Chapter
Three*

The King's Horses

Lala and her father stood quietly looking at each other. After a while her father spoke. He was very serious. "So you want the foal? You want it for your first horse. First horses are important. Last year your heart was set on owning a palomino."

"You did not have a palomino foal last year, Papá, remember? A mountain lion killed the mare. But you have this foal here now. I will take it gladly if you give it to me."

"Do you know enough about horses to own one?" he asked. Then looking teasingly at her, he said, "This foal is of a special breed, a descendant of one of the six Queen Isabella of Spain sent from her royal stables to our people of New Spain. They were her favorites. She wanted her subjects in the New World to breed them, also."

Lala laughed. "No, no, Papá. You cannot catch me in such a mistake about one of our horses. It was six palominos, the golden horses of Spain, that Queen Isabella sent. They were the ancestors of your Dorado, not of this foal. This foal is an Appaloosa."

"Appaloosa is an Indian word. Is this horse then an Indian horse?" her father asked, trying to hide his pleasure in what his daughter knew. Lala laughed again. "The Indian here in New Spain gave him that name because an Appaloosa is his favorite horse. But the Appaloosa is of Arabian stock. The Arabs brought it to Spain when they conquered us. It ran with the Lippizaner herds."

"How do you know this?" the Patrón asked, pleased but also puzzled.

"An Appaloosa runs with the Lippizaners in the big painting we have in the sala. Maman told me about it. She told me you bought the painting in Spain because you loved the Lippizaners."

For a second her father seemed lost in thought, then he said "Ay! Ay! Those Lippizaners! The most beautiful horses in the world! I will never forget them. I will dream of them always. My great-uncle took me to see them when I was a schoolboy in Spain. He took me to the Spanish Riding School in Vienna. Little One, you should have seen this riding school. It was a part of the palace of the Emperor of Austria. An immense hall with high white walls hung with draperies of crimson velvet and lighted by crystal chandeliers that reflected their lights in great mirrors framed in gold. You should have seen the horses! Unbelievable that anything that lived could be so beautiful. Statues in flowing movement! Ah, my Lalita, if I could have bred Lippizan horses, or even to own one's own Lippizaner! And to ride it as a Spaniard of Spain! That used to be my dream."

"Why can you not have one, Papá? The Conquistadors brought the Appaloosa to New Spain. Columbus brought the Barb. Ponce de León brought the quarter horse. Surely one of our Spaniards must have brought a Lippizaner."

The Patrón shook his head, "Not one. Not one was brought here. The reason I do not know, but not one came here."

"They breed them still in Austria. You could have one sent to you." Lala was puzzled. Her father was

33

known throughout the land for the horses he had bred. "You could build your own herd of the beautiful white horses."

The Patrón suddenly looked old, looked discouraged. "No," he said. "No more new horses. The day of the hacienda is over. It is passing quickly. For more than two hundred years my family have lived here, in this hacienda on this land grant given to us by the King of Spain. Two hundred years is a long time, little daughter."

Lala nodded. She felt so proud that her father talked to her as to a lady grown.

The Patrón continued. "We built slowly as the sons took wives and the grandsons in time also married and raised their children here. Now you see what has happened. There are empty patios without the songs and the laughter of children. My only son and my brother's sons are now in the States learning the ways of the North Americans."

Luis and Pita and 'Chacho looked into the distance. Lala looked at the foal.

The Patrón spoke again, "When my brother, the one you call Tío Toto, went outside to the States, taking your Tante Rita and his two sons and my son with him, then I knew the hacienda days were gone."

"But you sent Baptiste. You sent him to school." Tears clouded Lala's eyes and blurred her speech, but her father, intent on his own heartache, did not notice.

After a time, he continued. "The North Americans have taken the country. It may have been right that they took it. Certainly we were getting little from Mexico. No protection at all from Indian raids. The Americans have promised us protection. Of course, that is still to be proven. Our beautiful New Spain is called the Territory of New Mexico of the United States and your uncle goes to Washington to represent it." The Patrón spread his arms wide. "What else is there to do but educate one's son in the ways of the country that governs his land?"

A young Taos Indian came running from the wagon shed. "Patrón," he said, "with your permission, I speak." He was breathless with running and with excitement. "The Apache, Chief Canuto, is at the outer gate. He desires to enter."

"Does he come in friendship?" the Patrón asked.

"Yes, that is what he says. He says he has heard of the foal you have here. He wants to see it."

The Patrón laughed shortly. "Wants to steal it, or buy it if it cannot be stolen. However, if he says he comes in friendship, let him enter. But keep him outside the walls until the señorita Lala and I have had our morning ride."

Lala rode the pinto, sidesaddle as was proper. How she would have loved to be riding El Barb, astride, using her knees to guide him as the Moors had taught the Spanish to do, long ago.

The ride was a silent one. Often Papá sang as they rode together in the dawn of the morning, but not today. This morning her father's thoughts seemed far away. Lala would have liked to be sad with him, grieving for the day that sometime would be gone. But she could not be sad, not for long. Today her world seemed too beautiful and too wonderful for anyone to be sad. "I think I will soon own a horse," her heart sang, and she listened to it.

They rode around the circle pasture, bordered by the low foothills of the Sangre de Cristos on the banks of the Río. It was a blue and gold morning, Lala thought, blue in the distances and gold in the sunlight.

Clattering over the wooden planks of the bridge, they waved to José as he opened the water gate to let some of the river flow cascade into the lower level of the mother ditch.

Lala looked down at 'Chacho running at her pinto's side. She would have liked to tell him that she did not mind when he told Nana that she needed scoldings. This was what he was supposed to do. But 'Chacho, running, running, did not look up.

The young girl looked back at Luis, her father's major-domo. He was having difficulty keeping the Barb behind Papá's golden horse. It would be terrible if Luis let El Barb get ahead of Papá on the trail. Lala wished El Barb would get ahead. That would show Luis who could manage such a high-strung Arabian! But she knew that Luis would not let his mount go first.

They rode through the orchards of apricot and plum trees, of apple and cherry. Sunlight through the tree leaves made designs of light and shadow. A mockingbird mocked a quail call.

"Quoit, quoit, quoit, quoit," Lala sang back, teasing the mockingbird, mocking its mocking.

They rode by the grapevine rows and the bullhide wine vats kept under cover. No cloud marred the infinite blue sky above them. No jarring movement made a scar against the day's tranquillity. José had caught up with them diverting the water flow of the mother ditch into the little feeder ditches. This would

irrigate the milpa, where the young corn was growing. In between the corn rows grew the chili and the
bean plants.

To their right was the long, unbroken wall of the
hacienda. There were no windows in the outside
walls. Windows opened only on to inside patios. It
was difficult enough to guard barred gates and locked
doors and house roofs. Outside windows were a
luxury no hacienda could afford.

Riding now between the milpa and the house wall,
they faced another high adobe wall with a wide iron-
barred gate. Beyond the wall, Lala knew, was a
walled-in plaza and at its gate two high adobe towers.
The plaza was where hunters, trappers, muleteers,
freighters, soldiers, travelers made night camp on
their way along the Santa Fe Trail from Independence
to Taos and Santa Fe. The burro-laden caravans coming up the Royal Road from Mexico to Santa Fe and
Mora camped here also.

Her father's trading post was in this camp yard,
and his great warehouse stacked from floor to ceiling
with beaver pelts and sacks of wool. The big blacksmith and carpenter shop for the trail mules and
horses, for the wagons and stagecoaches, was built
between the warehouse and the mill with its great

water wheel turning slowly by the force of the acequia water flowing against it.

Between the mill wheel and the wall was a secret place. Once, last year, her brother Baptiste and her twin cousins Ricardo and Roberto told her that someday she might go there with them. From this high place, they said one could watch the covered wagons of the caravan lumbering through the gates of the two adobe towers. It was a small place, so small that only one at a time could squeeze into it, but taking turns, they could see much. It was a very secret place! She must never tell about it. The boys had made her promise not to tell about it. They had made her promise on a cross made with forefinger and thumb. She would need to take Pita, Lala thought, but she did not need to tell her about it. Taking her would be all that she needed to do. But 'Chacho, no. Never—if she could slip away from 'Chacho . . . Lala planned as they rode along.

When they reached the gate in the wall, they turned. The ride back would be along the way they had come; this was the only trail there was to ride. The land outside the walls and cedar-post fences was big and wide, but it was not a safe place. Enemy Indian bands might be hiding.

40

As they neared the corral, Lala saw that the foal was in the pen with its mother. She looked again. Beside the vaquero and the runner stood a tall, arrogant-looking Indian. It must be Canuto the Chief, Lala thought with excitement, her heart beating fast.

The vaquero and the runner were looking at the Indian. The Indian was looking at the foal, seemingly unaware of the hostility of those who watched him.

 *Chapter*
Four

Canuto, Indian Chief

The tall Indian was dressed in buckskin: buckskin jacket, fringed and beaded; fringed buckskin leggings; beaded buckskin moccasins. His black hair was almost shoulder-length, banded with a folded red kerchief. He was not on the warpath, Lala knew. Indians on the warpath had painted faces and were not hampered with buckskin clothing.

Lala looked at his horse. It, too, was buckskin, a buckskin pony, coffee-colored, with darker mane and tail. "Café-au-lait," Tante Rita called such a pony, always adding: "With a little sugar for its disposition, it might do for a trail-riding mount."

The buckskin stood quietly by the Indian's side.

43

"Tied to the ground," the vaqueros said when a horse had been trained to stand as if tied when its rein touched the ground. The horse was without saddle; Chief Canuto rode bareback always, disdaining a saddle. It was his boast that he could outrun and outride any vaquero in the land. Perhaps he could. He was a good rider and there were many fine horses in his herd.

The Patrón, dismounting hurriedly, spoke to the young Indian runner angrily, "I ordered you to have him wait outside the gates."

The boy was frightened, sensing the Patrón's anger. He tried to explain, speaking a mixture of his native language, Tigua, and Spanish: "But, Patrón, please, while I was telling him to stay outside he rode inside."

Lala's father turned to his daughter to help her dismount, but she had already slipped from her horse and was standing beside him. She spoke in French, suspecting that the Indian understood Spanish. "Will he harm the foal?"

Her father answered, also speaking French. He knew that Canuto understood and spoke Spanish perfectly. "No. Even if he could steal the foal, he would not harm it. He values good horses too highly."

45

"Will he steal it?" Lala tried to keep her voice steady, so that the Indian would not sense her fear.

The Patrón answered, also speaking lightly so that the red man would not sense his anxiety. "He will try, I think, but he will not be successful."

Satisfied for the moment with the answer, Lala turned bright-eyed attention to the Chief, who was still studying the foal, seemingly indifferent to the people and talk around him. She had heard of Chief Canuto many times. She knew that her father feared his deeds of cruelty and respected his courage. Lala had seen the Indian once before. As she rode in the stagecoach with her family along the road to Taos, the Chief and two of his warriors had ridden beside their carriage for a mile or two. The Indians were hunting antelope, her father had explained. Lala had peered out at them between the curtains of the coach door, but she did not see them very well.

Now she took a quick look at the tall, straight, proud-looking red man. He was taller than her father. He stood straighter—so stiffly straight, he looked as if when he moved, it would be to spring. Both men, the girl thought, had the same look of courage. Young as she was, she could recognize courage, and she had been taught to respect it.

46

Lala's look was interrupted. Her father told her, sharply, "Go to your mother at once."

"But I must wait for Pita," Lala said primly, her eyes still on the Indian. She knew where Pita was. Pita was huddled between two cedar posts of the corral fence. She had her rebozo wrapped tightly about her. Only her eyes could be seen, staring in terror at the wild Indian.

Lala avoided looking at her, saying to her father, "Maman desires that Pita accompany me, always. I cannot go without Pita."

"Pita is here beside you," the Patrón said, motioning the frightened Pita to move out of her hiding place. "Go, both of you. Go." There was nothing else to do but go. When Papá said "Go," one went. Lala tried to go with dignity.

Luis, glancing back, led El Dorado, El Barb, and the pinto to the far end of the corral. He, too, would have liked to stay to see what Canuto had to say, but he knew his responsibility was first for the horses' safety.

'Chacho did not give a backward glance as he followed the girls to the safety of the hacienda walls. The Indian was of no interest to him, but the safety of the señorita Lala was his life. He walked at the proper distance behind the two girls, but he wished they would hurry. He scowled at the back of Lala's head, trying to will her to hurry, but Lala walked slowly, much more slowly than usual. She said to Pita, "We are going because we have been told to go, but we will not run." Pita did not answer. She would have liked to run. She had seen what wild Indians were capable of doing. She had no wish to be near one.

At last they reached the doors of the wagon shed and walked by the forge and the carpenter bench and through the archway into the zaguán. 'Chacho was still scowling, but Lala dismissed him graciously as she had been taught to do, but with more than a hint of mischief in her sparkling black eyes.

It had been a good morning, Lala thought, a wonderful morning! Her father had talked with her as if she were a grown-up lady. She had touched the little foal and she thought her father planned to give it to her. She had seen close at hand the warrior Chief Canuto. Yes, it had been a good morning. She began to sing. Pita did not join her, but trudged along, a somber little figure wrapped in her rebozo. Lala, to make up for Pita's silence, sang louder, so that no one might know that only one was singing.

"Arre, mi burrito, que vamos a Belén,
Que mañana es fiesta y el otro también.
Arre, arre, arre, lléveme usted al trote,
Arre, arre, arre, lléveme al galope.
De prisa, de prisa."

Her mother, standing in the patio archway, called gaily: "You are late this morning, Little One. Where is your father?"

"Talking with Chief Canuto," Lala answered, as if talking with the Indian was an everyday pleasure.

Her mother gasped. "The Indian? The Indian Chief?"

"Have no fear, Maman. Papá is but a few steps behind me," Lala said happily, going to her room with Nana to change her dress for the breakfast meal.

Breakfast was served under the *portal* in the patio by the fountain. The roof of the *portal* gave shade, and the sun streaming down into the patio gave warmth—a pleasant combination, Lala thought, bowing her head as her father gave the blessing. When the family had been larger, and now when there was company, meals were served at the long, high table at one end of the kitchen. Lala liked eating under the *portal* with her mother and father best.

At most meals there was light talk, bantering and gay, between her parents, and she was brought delicately with laughing tenderness into the conversations. The bright flowers in the patio flower beds, the tinkling water falling into the fountain, the song of birds, and the laughter and talk made mealtimes in the patio less formal than meals served in the cool, dark kitchen. Then there were more people and small girls were less important.

Rosa, who helped María in the kitchen, served the breakfast. But from time to time María came in to see if the Patrón was eating with enjoyment and to look with affectionate disapproval at the Patrona's plate if the food on it was left uneaten. María was an Apache, tall and fat and wide. Lala was her pet, and the two had many little secrets, shared together.

The plates they used were of solid silver, the forks and spoons hand-hammered by the hacienda silversmith. The Patrón drank his chocolate from a heavy silver mug, but Lala liked hers in a thin, white porcelain cup. Maman, true to her French upbringing, drank coffee, which was mostly chicory, heavily sweetened with sugar.

Lala was hungry. The ride with her father and the excitement of seeing Canuto had made her hungry.

She ate with appetite the hot blue corn tortillas, wafer thin, and the cornmeal tamales stuffed with ground meat and chili and wrapped and boiled in cornhusks. There also was rice seasoned with saffron, and mashed fried beans. No meal was complete without fried bean paste.

This morning's breakfast was not as gay as usual. It almost was a silent meal. The Patrón seemed worried. Maman, sensitive to his mood, did not break in upon his silence. She guessed his worry. But not for the wealth of the Spanish crown would she let him know that Lala had told her Canuto had come inside the outer wall.

Lala also knew that her father was worried. And knew why he was worried. Added to this was her knowledge that Maman would eat in serene and smiling silence until her husband showed his willingness for talk.

Lala tried eating in silence. She had been taught that it was not for young girls to speak first in any situation. But there was something she must know. With a desperate look, she implored her mother to ask the question. Maman drank coffee and looked out at the fountain.

At last the little girl's curiosity got the better of

her manners. She asked the question. "Papá, Papá, please, what did Chief Canuto say about the foal?"

Her father looked at her briefly, "He said he liked it."

"Papá, will he plan to steal it, do you think?"

Her father raised his shoulders and his hands. "He offered to buy it."

"Will you sell the foal to him, Papá?"

The Patrón looked at his wife. His look said plainly: Can this child be a Spanish child, to question so rudely?

"No," he said shortly, bowing to his wife, asking to be excused. His day was long, his work unending. They would not see him again until early afternoon, when the heavy midday meal was eaten.

Maman sat quietly looking at Lala, waiting for an explanation.

"I had to know, Maman," Lala sobbed. "I had to know about the foal. I think Papá will give it to me, if nothing happens to it. The foal will be the first horse that I have owned. That is important."

Her mother said gently, "To own a horse, yes, that is somewhat important, but to love it is the very important thing."

"I love the foal," Lala insisted.

"No," her mother again corrected her. "Loving a horse comes slowly. It comes with mutual trust. It comes with companionship. It comes with the sharing of pleasures and dangers together."

"I know I'll never love another horse the way I love that foal," Lala said stubbornly.

Her mother laughed. "It is a small heart that has room for only one love, little daughter."

Suddenly Lala's smile came bursting like sunlight through a rain-heavy cloud. "Maman," she said softly, touching her mother's hand.

"Annette." And this time when her mother said "Annette" it sounded like a blessing.

 *Chapter
Five*

Hacienda Patrona

Lala went with her mother. She was expected to do, in a small-girl way, all the things considered the duties of the mistress of the hacienda. The hacienda Patrona organized and planned the running of her household. She trained and supervised, rewarded and punished the household servants as well as the paid workers of the household. She cared for them in health and in sickness, gave them sympathy in times of sorrow and made possible the celebrations of festive occasions for their pleasure.

A hacienda gathered its servants in many ways. They might have come as captives. They might have come as hostages. Many were born into the hacienda and wished to remain there. They were free to leave, but few left. There were many reasons for this. The hacienda was a happy place. The Patrón and the Patrona took care of its people. There was mutual love and loyalty. Besides, where else was there to go in the vast and empty land?

The work of the hacienda was never-ending for the Patrón, the Patrona, and all the workers. The hacienda had to be self-sufficient, making the things that were needed and doing the things that needed to be done. The work was patterned by the seasonal work needs of the year, emphasized and enlightened by the many fiestas, hampered and burdened by the many Indian raids.

There must be daily rounds for training, for supervision, for checking of supplies and equipment. There must be daily, loving contact with all the families.

This morning the Patrona went first into the kitchen patio. The sala across from the zaguán she would not visit today. It would need to be cleaned for the Fiesta of Saint John. Today she could pass it by.

The kitchen patio was a work patio. Here were no shady *portals*, no flower beds, no tinkling fountain. In the center was a well with its peaked-roof well house painted blue and its pulley and rope dangling two wooden buckets. On three sides the patio was enclosed by the walls of the kitchen and storerooms. Its arched opening, as in the other patios, led into the cobblestoned zaguán. Neither the kitchen nor the storerooms had shuttered windows, but high on the walls were openings grilled with straight, slender aspen.

The kitchen patio was a busy place. Carmen, on her knees before a stone metate on the hard earth floor, was rubbing dried chili peppers into powder—scolding, sneezing, wiping her eyes as she rubbed them. Rosa knelt before another metate. She was grinding corn kernels by rubbing them up and down with another stone. This was the first grinding, and after two more grindings the cornmeal would be powder-fine.

Rosa called to the Patrona, "Carmen wishes she were a Pueblo Indian so the young men would sing to her as she grinds."

"I could send her Tranquilino," the Patrona said.

Carmen made a face, but she was pleased to have been noticed. "That slow one!" she said, laughing.

The Patrona went on to test the heat of the adobe

57

ovens by the well house. "The heat is right," she
called to Lupe, who was kneading wheat-flour dough
in a huge wooden dough bowl. Lupe, who had been
daydreaming, began to hurry, pushing and patting
the dough into loaf shapes. With her thumb she in-
dented each top crust with a little cross.

"To make it bake good," she told Maman, who
smiled and waited for the loaves to be placed on flat
wooden trays.

Lupe cleaned the hot ashes of cedarwood from
the ovens, put the loaves of bread inside, and sealed
the openings. They would bake at leisure. She smiled
at Lala standing so quietly by her mother's side.

Next the Patrona examined the hollow cottonwood log that was used for a molasses press. Clean.
Good. It must stay this way. This was not the season
for molasses-making. There was tallow in the tallow
vat for candles and for soap. They would need many
candles for fiesta. The soap molds were empty. That
was as it should be. There still was a supply of soap.

The Patrona went into the cool, dark kitchen.
María went with her, squeezing Lala's hand as they
walked together. Her kitchen was kept in perfect
order, María thought. She intended that the Patrona
should be made aware of such perfection. "See the

brazier, Patrona. Its fire of cedarwood burns slowly, as I want it, to bring the olla of beans to perfect boiling."

The walls of the kitchen, black with years of smoke and the grease wafted upward from frying foods on the chimneyless brazier, looked like polished mahogany. Against it were hung the gleaming copper kettles. "Make note of the kettles, Patrona. It is I, not Rosa, who scours them with vinegar and sand."

There were a few iron pots and on the cutting table a few steel knives. These articles were both brought from the States by caravan. They were highly prized, much more so than the handmade copper kettles and the clay ollas used for cooking. Long-handled wooden spoons and wooden and gourd scoops of all shapes and sizes hung from the ceiling vigas at places convenient for using. "None missing," boasted María, pointing to them with pride. "None in need of a new thong to hang it by."

In the trastero were stored the silver plates and mugs, the porcelain cups and the majolica bowls, the wineglasses and decanters of crystal.

Lightly the young Patrona touched María's hand to show her that she was aware of and pleased with the perfection of the kitchen. María would treasure this light touch more than any words of praise. Of all the hacienda workers, María was the favorite of the Patrona. Nana, of course, was dear to her heart. But Nana she had brought with her when she had come as a bride to the house of her husband's family. How young she had been then, the Patrona thought. She had brought her dolls with her, which Nana, to please her, had dressed and sung to until Baptiste, the first born, had come to take their place.

How frightened she had felt that first year in the midst of her husband's large family of brothers and sisters and cousins. When Rita, her sister—younger by a year, but livelier and more fearless—had come as the bride of her husband's brother, she had been delighted. The two young French brides had learned together how to become Patronas of the hacienda in the traditional, formal manner of Spain. How young she had been then, she thought again. In many ways Lala was older at eleven years than she had been at fifteen.

She looked around for Lala. Lala was beside her as she was supposed to be, learning to do by watching it done.

Nana and Pita were in the patio outside, waiting to assist her when she needed them. They carried baskets, Nana's a very large one and Pita's somewhat smaller.

Finished with kitchen inspection, María led the way into the "little room of the sweets," where boiled corn, mashed, was made into tortillas. Here also were bundles of cinnamon sticks tied together and hung from the vigas, keeping company with clusters of dried raisins and strings of dried apples and apricots. On a high counter were trays of freshly made pan dulce and of little fried pies stuffed with mincemeat.

The Patrona motioned Pita to come with the basket she would carry for Lala, and to María to fill it with small amounts of everything in the room. These small treats Lala would take to the old and to the children of all the hacienda workers. Lala would be expected to dole them out with graciousness and prudence. Not lightly, but with thought. "A gift given lightly," Maman said, "was one to be valued lightly."

The basket filled, Pita put it on her head. This was the way she would carry it when they went to the homes of the hacienda people. Neither Lala nor Pita looked at each other, nor did they speak. This was worktime. During worktime Lala was the Little Patrona and Pita was the little girl being trained to serve her. Worktime was not playtime. Pita would have been embarrassed if Lala was so unknowing as to speak with her of unnecessary things during their hours of working together.

Before they left the "little room of the sweets," the Patrona looked into the ollas of molasses and the ollas of mincemeat. She examined the bundles of sugar cane. She nodded. She was satisfied. María and the others trailed her from the room.

The next door opening on to the kitchen patio was the wine room, where the hacienda-made wines and brandies were kept in bullhide kegs. This room was kept locked. Maman unlocked the door with one of the large iron keys hanging in a key ring from her sash belt. The room was damp, with the musty, sweet smell of fermented grapes. The Patrona looked at each bullhide keg with its sealed cover and its bung-hole securely corked. One was leaking drop by drop onto the hard earth floor. The Patrona was outraged. María was aghast.

"This cannot have happened. It is not possible that it should happen," María wailed, tightening the cork and fingering the wet spot on the floor.

Lala wanted to laugh. There was such horror on Maman's face and on María's. Their faces almost looked alike, although Maman's face was young and beautiful and María's was jolly-looking and fat. Quickly Lala looked away from Maman, María, and the wet spot on the floor. A small Patrona did not laugh while she was being trained to be a real Patrona later on when she was older.

They passed through the storeroom where the grains were kept and then through the large, cool room where the meat was stored.

The last storeroom, bordering the kitchen patio, was the herb room. The Patrona was tired, but this was only the beginning, for the long hours lay ahead. In this room Nana's basket would be filled.

Here were the dye plants for the yarns that the women in the weaving room would soon be needing. The Patrona checked her memory. The sheep had been sheared. The wool had been washed and carded in batts. The women were spinning now. Soon the great copper kettles must be filled with dye plants and water and boiled over little out-of-door fires. Hanks of the spun wool would be dipped in the dye kettles and redipped and dipped again until they took on the color that the weavers wanted. Then they would be hung on the drying lines and turned with the sun for even drying.

Lala loved to go into the patio when the yarns

were drying. They looked like bits of a rainbow hung out to dry. She stepped closer to her mother so she could see the dye plants that were selected. Her mother made slow, careful, deliberate selection. Chamiso for yellow. Lichen for gray-green, the color of river water in the evening light. Mountain mahogany for rich red-brown. Maman chose balls of indigo. The weavers always wanted blue color, and the only blue to be had was from indigo. It had to be brought by muleback up the Royal Road from Mexico. Maman put six balls of indigo in the basket Nana would carry. Then she measured a small quantity of cochineal powder. The weavers liked this powder because it dyed their yarns a pleasing cochineal red. It was made of a tiny insect that fed on cactus. The Indians of Mexico and Guatemala picked by hand each small insect and by a long slow process made the powder. It, too, was freighted up the Camino Real and, like indigo, was expensive.

Maman thought for a while, planning ahead for the cloth, the blankets, and floor rugs that would need to be woven in the months to follow. She decided that she had chosen enough dye plants and minerals and powder.

Now she turned her attention to the medicinal

herbs that she should take with her today when she made the rounds of all the houses of the workmen.

There would be need of all that she could take. There was always need. There were always the sick: some with the chills and fever they had brought with them from their homeland far to the south; some with the aches and miseries that seemed to be the crown of age. There were many who were old and nearing the end of their life of labor, but also there were many young to take the old one's places. To the medicines in Nana's basket the Patrona added little cheesecloth bags of dried lavender, rosemary, and some rose petals. A whiff of these fragrances, Maman knew, was often an antidote for pain.

At last they were ready to go. This was the part that Lala liked, visiting the workers in their little workrooms and in their houses. Lala knew all of them by name, knew that she loved them and that they loved her. They were part of the hacienda family, as she was part of it. The workers labored for the Patrón and his family, and the Patrón and his family took care of the workers in childhood and in old age, in sickness and in health. This was the way of life. From Mexico into northern New Mexico it had been strong and tight for hundreds of years, and only a few knew that its day in history was ending.

66

Lala and her Mother walked in dignity down the long zaguán. Nana and Pita followed, jauntily, proudly, their laden baskets on their heads. They were the ones close to the young, beautiful Patrona and to her happy-hearted little daughter. They were the chosen ones.

 **Chapter
Six**

Work of the Day

On one side of the long zaguán was the sala, the
patio with the fountain, the chapel, and the sleeping
rooms for Lala, her parents, and her brother Baptiste
when he was home. On this side, too, were three
other patios with an archway opening on to the
zaguán and three walls with *portal*-shaded rooms. All
the rooms opened on to the patio. None of them
had connecting doors. There were many patios and
many rooms because they had been needed when the
family was large. They were also needed for visitors.
When visitors came, it was for at least ten days. And
the whole family would come: the parents, a grand-

69

parent or two, a great-grand aunt perhaps, the brothers and sisters, aunts, uncles, and cousins, and always as many household servants as they could squeeze into the square carretas. The family rode in coaches drawn by spans of mules. Sometimes they brought their riding horses. There must be room for all and for everything.

Opposite the sala on the other side of the zaguán were the kitchen and the storerooms, the craftmen's workrooms and the work patios. At the back, in a long line, were the houses of the workmen. All these were within the hacienda walls. There were other walls and tight fences of cedar posts, but all the people slept inside the hacienda walls.

Today the Patrona planned to visit only the work patios and workrooms and the workers' houses. The patio rooms would have to wait until the week when they were cleaned and made ready for the Patrón's name day, the Fiesta of San Juan Bautista.

The Patrona went first to the work patio next to the kitchen and the storerooms. This was where the hacienda craftsmen had their little stalls and work-benches, the simple equipment and supplies they needed, and each had his clay brazier and his little tin lantern housing his own particular saint.

She stopped first at the shoemaker's work place.

The shoemaker made botas and leggings for the men and the sandals that the women and the children wore. He made bags and straps and bridles and could if the occasion demanded turn out a buckskin coat or a fitted leather vest. The Patrona sent to France for her own slippers and for Lala's, but they needed sandals for everyday wear, and so it seemed did almost all the other women and children. The list was a long one and the shoes would be needed before the summer was ended. "Too many sandals," the shoemaker grumbled, but he was pleased. It was good to know that he was the one who would keep all of them sandaled or barefoot. Lala had a cluster of raisins to give him, not from the basket, but from a fold in her sash. "Because," she told him, "this is for you only." He smiled at Lala and said to the Patrona: "But have no fear. The sandals will be made long before summer's ending."

The cabinetmaker, next to the leather worker, did fine carpentry, carving and painting in intricate designs the panels of doors and chest drawers, the legs of tables and the headboards of beds and high backs of benches. He had made Lala's carved bed. He asked her this morning, as he asked her every morning, if she had enjoyed, last night, the sweet dreams he had carved for her in its design.

Maman had no work for him this morning, but she knew that if she did not stop to talk with him his feelings would be hurt. She told him, "You will have so much work getting ready for Saint John's Day that it is well to let your hands be idle this little while."

The remark displeased him. "Idle! My hands are never idle, with that María always breaking furniture in your kitchen."

The Patrona smiled at him and he forgave her.

"She is beautiful," he told the shoeman.

"And good," the shoeman answered.

"Sí, sí, and good," the cabinetmaker agreed.

The old candlemaker sat asleep in the morning sunshine. "Let the poor little one sleep," the Patrona said gently. "Next week her poor hands will ache with dipping candles for fiesta."

The next work stall, belonging to Adrian, the French hairdresser, had its own door. Monsieur Adrian had insisted on having a door to his workroom when he had first come many years ago from France to do the hair of the two French girls from Taos. The girls, now grown to women, had adored Monsieur Adrian, knowing that he kept their puffs and pompadours and curls in the latest fashion. But now his door was closed and padlocked.

73

Tante Rita had taken him to the States, insisting that she had to have him. "He is a necessity. It is not possible to go without him," she had stormed, using her hands, her shoulders, and her flashing eyes to punctuate her sentences. Being the younger sister and also the wife of the younger brother, she had her way. Monsieur Adrian had gone to Washington. Maman always gestured in irritation when she passed the closed, padlocked door. It was a necessity that her hair also be kept in the latest fashion, she thought, walking a little faster. Not perhaps for every day, but certainly for fiestas.

Lala hurried to keep up with her mother. The next workroom was her favorite place, and Old Ramón her special friend. Old Ramón was a Mexican silversmith of great age, and greatly gifted. It was he who hand-hammered the forks and spoons and sand-cast the plates and platters. But what he liked best was the making of gold-filigree necklaces, and combs and earrings.

"I fashion my dreams in filigree," he told the small girl, and he showed her a high comb of tortoise shell and gold. "This is a name-day gift," he said, "to hold high the mantilla of a certain little lady."

She knew—she thought she knew—the comb would

be for her on Saint Anne's Day. She answered gravely, "The little lady cannot help but like it, señor. It is of great beauty."

Maman called her to hurry. They were at the last workroom, the room of Tío Tony, as everyone called him. He was now the hacienda troubadour, the song-maker and teller of tales. Almost five years ago he had come riding up the Camino on a thin little burro, carrying his handmade violin and his copybook of song. He had come for the night, he had told the Patrón. "I can give you my songs for only the night that is coming. Then I must be on my way. A minstrel dares not tarry on the trail. He travels the world!" But he had stayed, always planning to go on after one more night.

Now he was sick. "Very sick," he told the Patrona.

"Where?" she asked.

"Ah, Patrona, that you ask a troubadour where his sickness lies! It travels. Sometimes here. Sometimes there."

Would he like tansy tea? "Yes, Patrona, and mint tea also and a bit of a poultice if you have one, and chocolate, Patrona."

Maman looked in her basket. No chocolate! She had forgotten the chocolate.

"A bit of chocolate would have cured me," he told them sadly as they left him.

At the houses of the workmen Maman gave out the medicines and the poultices and the bags of fragance. She gave words of encouragement and praise and words of sympathy. Each where the need was.

The children crowded around Lala. Before she knew what was happening, her basket was empty. Now she had nothing left to give Blind Juana, who sat in the sun all day because she had nothing else to do. Lala's eyes filled with tears. Her mother looked at her and looked away. The little one must learn, she thought, to give with judgment, remembering all who must be given something.

Lala fought her tears. To cry would disgrace all of them. A Patrona wiped other people's tears. She did not shed them. Not where the workers and their children could see her. Then she felt Nana's wrinkled hand against her own clenched fist. Nana was giving her a little piece of chocolate. Nana, it seemed, also kept special treats in the folds of her sash. Lala smiled at Nana through her tears and put the sweet bit in the blind woman's hand. Blind Juana fingered it, saying, "Well, something is better than nothing."

Maman still looked at the archway tiles, but Lala knew that she had seen both the giving and the gift. Chocolate! The knowledge brought comfort to the shame of having one's basket emptied too soon.

The spinning room was the last place to visit. Lala thought that always Maman chose it to be last because it was such a happy place. This early afternoon the women were singing to their babies as they spun the carded wool into huge balls of yarn. They were singing an old Spanish lullaby sung by mothers to their babies since Oñate had brought the first Spanish women to help colonize New Spain.

> *"Sleep, little one,*
> *Sleep, little baby.*
> *For your night cradle*
> *I give you my heart."*

Lala looked at the sleeping babies and at their mothers spinning and weaving. They were her people, French and Spanish, Mexican and Indian. How much she loved them!

When the Patrona finished her work in the spinning room, the women began a new song. This was an old Pawnee song that was sung to babies when their fathers were on the warpath. No one knew

77

where the women in the spinning room had learned the song. There were no Pawnee among them. They were Mexican Indians and Indians from New Mexico, not from the Plains.

But now they were singing it, as always they sang it when they were uneasy, when there was rumor of Indian raid.

> *"Ho Hahars, thy baby is crying,*
> *grieving and wailing and weeping.*
> *Ho Hahars sirah ti wera."*

Maman and Lala, Nana and Pita walked in the wide, cool zaguán. They had left more than basketfuls of poultices and sweet bits. They had left devotion and laughter. Most times Lala was aware of this, and because of it her heart was filled with happiness. But not today. She knew why the women sang the Pawnee song. She knew and she was worried. She felt her mother's hand in hers. Her mother began to sing:

> *"Ho Hahars, sirah ti wera.*
> *Thy father is coming.*
> *Even now he is near thee.*
> *Cry no more. Cry no more.*
> *Ho Hahars sirah ti wera."*

78

The people hurrying back and forth in the zaguán smiled at her, and one by one they began to sing:

"Ho Hahars sirah ti wera."

All the hacienda was filled with the song.

*Chapter
Seven*

Day's End

The midday meal, eaten in the early hours of the afternoon, was a long one and a heavy one. The food was served in courses: soup, roasted chicken, boiled mutton with onions, beef boiled with corn and chili, fried rice with saffron, fried bean paste, blue-corn tortillas, wheat-flour bread, and dried fruits. Lala thought the meal would never end. She was tired and sleepy.

Her parents talked of the coming feast day of San Juan Bautista. Aside from Christmas, Easter, and the Feast of Guadalupe, it was the most important fiesta of the year for the hacienda. It was the name day of the Patrón and the son of the Patrón, though Lala's brother was called by the French form of the name, Baptiste. This year would be the first year that Baptiste would not share with his father the honors of the day.

Lala knew that this grieved her parents. She, too, missed her brother, and she missed the cousins, Roberto and Ricardo. She missed their good companionship, their gay teasing, and their fun-loving ways. Along with missing them, Lala envied them a little. They had seen beyond the walls of the hacienda and the mountains of the Sangre de Cristos. They had gone outside. They had gone to Washington in the States.

What was Washington like, she wondered. Was it like Mexico City or New Orleans or Quebec? Was it like Paris or Seville? Not that she had seen those cities. She had not been taken farther than Taos and Santa Fe. But she knew about them. In the sala were books with pictures of these cities. She knew that her mother's mother had come from France to New Orleans, and her mother's father from Quebec to New Orleans. Together they had come to Taos, bringing her mother and her aunt. Her mother had told her stories about New Orleans. Her father shared with her his memories from his school years in Spain. But it was the troubadour who had made the cities live. He had known their glitter and their glory, and from this knowledge he made his songs and he sang them to her.

She strung the cities in a silent little thread of song: "Quebec and Mexico City, Paris and New Orleans and Seville, where the roses grow." She had asked the troubadour about the new one, Washington, but of Washington he did not know. But he planned to go there, he said, tomorrow or next week when he took to the road again. Lala wondered how it would feel to be a troubadour and travel the roads of the world or be a boy and get to go to school in Washington.

Her daydreaming was interrupted by Luis, who brought a packet for Papá that had come by special messenger. Lala forgot that she was tired. She forgot that she was sleepy. She forgot that young girls spoke only when they were spoken to.

"Letters, Papá? Are they letters? Are they from Baptiste or the primos? Perhaps Tante Rita or Tío Toto have written to us."

"Yes to all your questions," her father laughed, sorting out the letters and giving them to Maman and to Lala, keeping some for himself.

Papá's letters were written in Spanish, Maman's in French.

"And yours?" they asked Lala.

"Mine is from Baptiste," Lala answered sadly, "but it is in English and I cannot read it."

"Have I not told you," her father said, "that you should work with diligence when your mama teaches you English?" Lala looked at her mother through her thick long eyelashes. Not for a serape full of emeralds would she tell Papá that Maman taught her much French, enough Spanish. But English not at all.

Her father saw the look and knew its reason. He was amused. "Give the letter to me, my little dunce," he told her. "I will read it to you."

The letters, which they read and shared, had in them good news, but also bad news. Tío Toto was coming on business of the government to Santa Fe. Tante Rita would come with him and they would stop for a day at the hacienda. They would try to arrive for Saint John's Day, but if that were impossible they would come for a certainty for the Fiesta of Saint Anne, the name-day fiesta for Annette, which was Lala's real name.

This was the good news, the good, wonderful news. They were coming!

The bad news was bad. It was bad for the people of the hacienda. The three boys were not coming with Tante Rita and Tío Toto. Their trip would be a hurried one, the visit at the hacienda short. The papers that Tío Toto carried were papers of government. There was need for haste. Maman looked sad. She missed her son. Even for a day she would want to see him. Papá looked at her with affection and understanding. He, too, would have liked to see his son.

Then came more good news. Tío Toto was asking permission that Baptiste accompany his sons to Spain and France. Monsieur Adrian would go with them. At least it was good news for Baptiste and Ricardo and Roberto. Maman's hands made a little flying gesture of annoyance. Not only would she not see Baptiste, but it would be another year before she had her hair done properly again. "Monsieur Adrian to go with them," she said with irritation.

The Patrón smiled. He remembered, as he had called it, the Tempest in the Teapot over which sister should have the services of Adrian. He said mildly, "We must talk together about this permission for Baptiste to go." But he knew, both of them knew, that Baptiste would go. It was the pattern of the day to send the sons for schooling back to the Mother Country.

Lala also knew that Baptiste would go. She said hopefully, "Perhaps now that he will be gone so long, he will make me a gift of El Barb. It is his horse so it would be proper for him to give it."

Nana touched her shoulder. "If the Patrona permits, it is time for the señorita's siesta."

"It is time for siesta for everyone," Maman said, rising. "We have kept María and Nana and Rosa from their rest time."

Nana did not speak, but she agreed with Maman. It was past the time for beginning siesta. Everyone— everyone went to sleep for three hours after the heavy midday dinner. This was the hacienda pattern, the hacienda way of life. Even the parrots slept on their patio perches.

Lala planned to stay awake. She had no time for sleeping just because it was siesta time: she had too many things to think about. The most important, of course, was the foal. She wanted to experience again in memory how wonderful it had been to touch it. She knew that to pet and fondle a colt was the first act in its training. Perhaps Papá would give it to her for her name-day gift. There might be a palomino later, when the chestnut mare foaled, but the Appaloosa foal was here now. To own a horse, she thought. To own a horse! It was foolish to think that Baptiste would give her El Barb. He would keep it. If she ever got the Appaloosa foal, she would keep it forever.

The room was cool and dark and still. Sleep gathered her in the folds of its silence. Her damp curls were very black against the whiteness of the pillow. Nana looked at the small girl with tenderness. Such a little spitfire and such a little lady, so mischievous and so loving. So French and yet so Spanish. "What will the gringos do to her," the old Indian woman mumbled as she fastened the shutters against the wall and turned the key in the lock.

Sun, which was the hacienda clock, moved slowly in majesty across the cloudless sky. The people of the hacienda slept. The vaqueros slept almost under the hooves of the horses they were guarding. José, in the shadow of the corn rows, slept by the trickle of water in the little feeder ditch.

Gradually the sun reached the western skyline, turning the red earth of the foothills of the Sangre de Cristo to darker crimson and at last flaming the sunset sky with tongues of gold and scarlet.

87

Nana wakened Lala. It was time for merienda, when she, Maman, and Papá had sweet cakes, and honey cakes and chokecherry jam to eat as they drank thick chocolate, frothy and sweet. Evening shadows lengthened. Tranquilino came to shut off the stream of water in the fountain. Rosa and Carmen and Lupe lighted the candles in the tin and copper sconces on the whitewashed walls of the sleeping rooms, the zaguán, and the chapel. The evening star shone down on the fountain that now had no ribbon of water.

Softly, thin and clear, Rafael rang the little bell above the chapel door, calling the people of the hacienda to evening prayer. Slowly the workers came, walking up the wide, cobblestoned zaguán. They came in family groups, the old ones of the family, the younger parents, the children and babies. As they came walking, they came talking, laughing, with here and there a flash of song. They had labored and rested and eaten. Now they would give thanks to their Creator for this good day that He in His wisdom and mercy had bestowed upon them. In their coming to the chapel at twilight there was no system of high and low, of servant and served. The paid worker came with the hostage and the captive,

Indian and Mexican, Spanish and French, all those housed within the protecting walls bound together with the bonds of need and loyalty, of gratitude and devotion.

The chapel was small, but large enough to hold its people. There were no pews, no kneeling benches. The people knelt on the hard-packed earth that made the floor. The altar was simple and of exquisite beauty, hand-fashioned, hand-carved by hacienda workers from a young pine that had its roots deep in hacienda land. The altar cloth, with its wide edgings of handmade lace, was hand-spun and hand-woven. Golden candelabra filled with hand-dipped candles lighted and softened the figure of the crucified Christ which hung above the altar on the white-washed wall.

At the foot of the altar knelt the Patrón and the Patrona and Lala, and beside them, behind them, around them knelt their people. The Patrón, father of the hacienda, led his hacienda childern in prayer.

"God the Father of Heaven."

"Have Mercy on us."

"God Redeemer of the World."

"Have mercy on us."

There was a breath of silence, then a gasp of fear.

The big bell above the little bell outside the chapel was ringing out in shrill and frightening warning. "Indios, Indios," whispered the men as they ran from the chapel, across the patio, and down the candle-lit zaguán on swift and silent feet. "Indios, Indios," wailed the women in the chapel. "Indios, Indios," whimpered the children, drawing their rebozos tighter, hiding their faces in their mother's skirts. "Indios," shrieked the parrots, flapping their wings, climbing and hanging on their patio perches.

The Patrona still knelt at the foot of the altar. She did not move as her husband left her. She did not move as Lala crept closer to her. Her gaze was on the crucifix on the chapel wall. Her calm, beautiful voice did not tremble, did not falter, filled the chapel, calmed the frightened women.

"Ave Maria, pray for us.

Madre de Diós, pray for us."

Gradually the women joined her in prayer.

"Ave Maria. Ave Maria.

Mother of God."

Carmen, kneeling by the chapel door, shrieked in fury as a lighted firestick was thrown over the patio wall. "No water in the fountain," she screamed as she ran to put out the flame. "Where is that Tranquilino and his 'trickle of water'?"

90

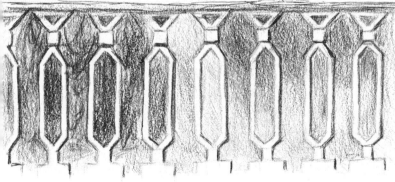

María stood beside her, dousing the burning wand with an olla of water. The Patrona smelled the burning wood but she did not turn her head. Not even her heartbeat must betray her terror, or the women whose safety was her responsibility would panic, would run to their husbands outside the house walls.

Still kneeling beside her mother, Lala began to cry. "They've taken my foal. They have stolen the poor little baby."

Immediately Nana was beside her. "Hush," she commanded sternly, but her arms were loving as she gathered the little girl close to her heart.

Carmen, Rosa, and Lupe stood at the patio arches with ollas of water, as María, striding up and down, a figure of fury, commanded them where to pour it.

An hour passed by. The women still prayed in the chapel. The children slept on the benches beside them. The parrots preened themselves on their perches.

At last the Patrón came back. He helped the Patrona from the floor, where erect and proud she had knelt the eternity of waiting.

"My beloved one," the Patrón whispered to her. He held his arms wide for Lala to come close to his heart. "Your foal is safe."

92

He looked at the women. "My children," he said aloud, "your husbands, your sons are safe. Go to them. Comfort them. Cherish them. The good God has spared them this night."

The women, crying softly, kissed his hand and, tired, yet with swift insistence, went down the zaguán to their waiting men.

 **Chapter
Eight**

Day of the Caravan

"We are here!" Lala said breathlessly, but in triumph. "Dear Pita, we are here." She laughed, trying to coax at least a smile from the shaking Pita. "Are you not glad that we are here?"

"No," wailed Pita. "We will be punished."

Lala answered cheerfully, "Of course we will be punished, if we are discovered, or," she added, trying to sound fierce, "if you should tell."

Pita was offended. "I will never tell, but my mamá will find out. Her punishment for us will be something terrible."

"Yes," Lala agreed. "All the more reason for us to enjoy ourselves now."

Lala sat on the ground, resting her head against the wall where the mill wheel turned endlessly. She needed to get her breath to prepare herself for the next feat, which would be climbing the wall to the hole near its top. For a year she had planned that on this day she would do this thing. At last the day had come. She was doing what she had planned to do. Everything was happening according to her plan.

The excitement of today had begun the evening before, when the call had gone through the hacienda. "Caravana! Caravana!" María had come running to Maman with the news. "They are here, Patrona. The Mexican traders from the Outside Country are here. They have come, Patrona. Even now they wait with their strings of pack burros at the outer gates."

That had been news of great importance. Mexican traders from the Outside Country! For this alone, Lala would have come to the place-in-the-wall, but added to this, there had come promise of even greater excitement. Long before this morning's sunrise, everyone in the hacienda knew that the Caravan of the Santa Fe Trail had night-camped but a half day's distance away. With the rising sun, the watches on the rooftop could see the billowing clouds of dust made by the lumbering oxen pulling the covered wagons along the deep ruts of the trail. By midmorning surely, the watchers said, the wagon train would have arrived at the plaza before the trading post.

Two caravans at once, one from the States, the other from Mexico! It was difficult to believe such a wonderful thing. Two caravans at once! The string of pack burros and their trader drivers came only occasionally and never on schedule. The caravan from the States came once a year. It took nine months to make the journey of almost nine hundred miles. Counting the time for layovers for repairs of the enormous wagons, the Patrón expected them about the time they came, except when, as sometimes happened, the train was looted and burned by raiding Indians. But to have both burro train and caravan at once did not happen often.

"This is truly a miracle," Lala, resting against the wall, told Pita. Pita would not sit, would not rest, would not look at Lala but stood ready to run if need be or to climb the wall if she was told that she must climb it. "Truly a miracle," Lala repeated. She clapped her hands in delight. What a day it would be!

At sunrise, as Nana had chosen the dress that she would wear and had brushed the tangles from her curls, Lala had known that everything would happen as she wanted it to happen. So far, the events of the day had been true to its promise.

The foal, when she went into its pen, acted as if it knew her. Papá, standing beside his golden Dorado, was waiting for her. Luis was riding Casi and not El Barb this morning. She and Papa sang together as they rode into the bright blue morning. It was a wonderful beginning.

At breakfast Maman told Papá what she wanted from the caravan. She herself, she told him, would deal with the Mexican traders, but he must select the things the Americans brought. First on her list were panes of Pittsburgh glass for the sala windows. There had never been glass in the windows of the hacienda, only shutters. But Rita was coming, Maman explained, and Rita had written that windows in the houses of Washington had glass. Therefore, the sala windows must have glass. Maman said that she was certain Papá would understand the need for Pittsburgh panes of glass. Papá nodded. He understood. Also, and for the same reason, the sala must have a Brussels carpet for its floor. Papá nodded. Besides these small extras, there were the dresses she had ordered sent from Paris and the slippers to match, for both herself and Lala. The list was a long one. Maman

98

was very gay, asking in a pretty fashion for the things she thought so necessary. Papá was pleased. Nothing made him happier than making Maman gay.

Breakfast over, Maman, with Nana at her side tightly clutching the big leather purse filled with silver coins, called for Carmen, Rosa, and Lupe. María, with key in hand, was stationed at the great doors of the zaguán by the sala. Her duty was to let in, one at a time, a Mexican trader and his heavily laden burro. Each trader was escorted into and out of the zaguán by Chacho, José, Pacho, or Tranquilino.

The trader unloaded his burro for Maman to inspect his wares, praising loudly each article that he had to sell. Then began the bargaining. No trader would think of selling anything in his pack at the first, second, or third price he put upon it. Neither would the Patrona have considered buying anything at the first, second, or third price put upon it. Aided by exclamations of outrage, from Carmen, Rosa, and Lupe, at the cost and at the dubious quality of the things for sale, Maman bargained. Centavo by centavo the prices came down. Almost at the same instant that the trader decided that this price was his lowest and his last, Maman decided that this was the best

price she could get. The trader wailed at the way he was being cheated. Lupe, Carmen, and Rosa wailed at the way he had cheated the Patrona. Nana doled out coin by coin in reluctant payment. Then Chacho, José, Tranquilino, or Pacho escorted the trader and his burro out the door in scowling disapproval of the way he had cheated the Patrona. Another trader and his overladen burro were brought in, and bargaining began anew.

Lala had seen many traders with many burros brought into the zaguán of the hacienda, and each time she was wide-eyed with the treasures the small beasts of burden had carried up the Royal Road from countries far to the south.

Lala and Pita gazed in silent wonder at the riches in the burro packs. There were lace mantillas from Spain and embroidered shawls from China and laces from France. There were preserved fruits and dried oysters and spices from the Caribbean countries. There were dyes from Central America and buttons and bells and bridles and bits from Mexico.

After a while Maman had purchased all the things that Lala thought were interesting. Then the burros loaded with metates, copper kettles, clay ollas and tinajas were brought in.

101

Lala decided the time had come for the real adventure of the day. "Maman," she said politely, "with your permission Pita and I will go. We are tired, having looked at so many things."

Her mother stopped briefly. "Yes, you may go. Get the colcha you are embroidering and I will measure the amount you must complete by dinnertime."

Lala had not expected to be given work that must be done, but she brought the colcha to her mother. She comforted herself with the thought that the place-in-the-wall was too small for two at the same time. While one of us looks, the other one can embroider, Lala thought, smiling gayly at her mother.

Such a happy little girl, Maman thought, going back to bargaining.

Pita took the colcha from the Patrona, folded it neatly, and put it on her head to carry to the patio by the fountain. But Lala motioned her to follow, not to the patio but down the zaguán. Pita's eyes were very big as she walked sedately behind her small Patrona. Where were they going, she wondered, surprised that they did not sit in the shade of the *portal* by the fountain.

The zaguán was a busy place, with burros and traders and workers milling around like moths at lighted candles. It was a noisy place, with traders shouting at their burros, and Tranquilino, Pacho, José, and Chacho shouting at the traders, and Lupe, Rosa, and Carmen helping their Patrona to bargain. María added to the noise by shouting: "Come in. Come in. Hurry. Hurry." And then: "Go out. Go out. Hurry. Hurry." Nana doled out the coins in small piles. She had neither eyes nor ears for anything else but the money in the money bag and the traders' demands for it. They must not get a cent too much, or too little. Poor things, Nana thought, walking all those hot and weary miles, but not too much. Never too much! No one noticed two little girls walking down the wide zaguán.

When they went through the wagon shed and out into the wide pasture, Pita's worry turned to horror. Lala walked along quietly but quickly. She knew that if she turned around, Pita would beg her not to go. So she did not turn around, even though her heart was beating wildly. Never before had she been outside the hacienda walls without Papá waiting, or her brother and cousins being with her, or Chacho to guard her. But she would not turn back. She was going to see the caravan in all its splendor.

At last they reached the outside wall. Lala was

103

breathless. Pita was shaking. "Poor little Pita. Poor little one," Lala comforted, but then added quickly, "Now you will climb up to the place where the mill wheel turns. Put the colcha in a safe place and be ready to help me if I need help." Pita looked up at the wall, looked back at the way they had come, then looked at Lala. There was a moment of silence.

Lala, wrapping her rebozo around her waist, climbed the wall. The hole was still there, as smooth and solid as it had been a year ago. Now, as then, it was large enough for only one to squeeze into. The wall was of adobe and very thick. When Lala wriggled in, she was lost completely from the view of the frightened Pita at the foot of the wall. Lala looked out into the plaza. "Oh, oh," she said softly in delight at what she saw.

The milling people in the zaguán were as nothing compared with the milling people, burros, mules, and horses before her father's post. Lala looked at the burro strings first. It was so much more exciting to see the burro strings here than it had been to see them in the zaguán, one trader and one burro at a time. Quickly Lala counted them. There were ten burros in a string and about a dozen strings. For each string there was a burro driver, who was a very noisy fellow, shouting at his companions and yelling at his burros. The lead burro of every string had a bell tied around its neck. The noise and confusion were wonderful!

She would look at one thing at a time, she decided. Then she would give Pita her turn. She took another quick look. Yes, of a certainty, it was much more exciting to see them here than one by one in the zaguán.

Lala wriggled out of the hole-in-the-wall and called down to Pita. "It is your turn now. I will reach down and help you climb up." Pita was still standing at the foot of the wall, and she had not taken the colcha from her head. "Come, Pita. It's the most wonderful sight you ever will see." But Pita stood unmoving. Lala slid down from the wall. "Well, if you won't look, I will and you can do my embroidery. I am giving you a choice." Pita took the colcha from her head, sat as close to the wall as she could, and began to embroider. Lala climbed the wall again.

The wagon trains were lumbering through the gate. Each wagon train had a lead wagon and three trailers. "Mules are pulling them," Lala said in surprise. Tranquilino had said there would be oxen. "One has to see for oneself," she said with satisfaction. She counted the mules. It took sixteen mules to pull one train. The lead mules, like the lead burros, had bells tied around their necks. The wagon-train driver did not walk beside his sixteen mules. He rode the nigh mule, which was saddled, and commanded his train from there with firmness and great skill. "I'd like to ride a nigh mule of a wagon train. I know I could."

She tried to count the wagons. "There must be at least twenty-five." What a sight to see! The wagons were canvas-covered, long and narrow, with the back wheels higher than the front ones. I wonder why that is, she thought. There would be no one she could ask. "Perhaps I will never know," she said aloud, leaning down to look again at Pita. "It's your turn now, Pita." Pita did not look up. Her slender brown fingers moved swiftly, stitching the design with blue yarn on the soft white wool coverlet. "I am going to look once more," Lala promised. "Then we will go back within the walls." Pita did not look at her. Lala felt hungry. It must be time, almost, for the midday meal. Only one more look, but she must see everything.

This time Lala looked at the people. There must be a hundred, moving around, talking together, shouting at the mules and burros. Only the Indians at the edges of the crowd remained unmoving. They sat on their horses like statues, but Lala knew they saw everything. She drew back into the hole, a little afraid and yet determined to see. There were many scouts and hunters, dressed in fringed and beaded buckskin. They had come to sell and to buy. The Mexican traders wore white cotton, the hacienda workers from her father's and from neighboring haciendas wore khaki-colored homespun. The mule drivers wore blue jeans. They were the first blue jeans she had ever seen and were from the States. She looked at them approvingly. The wagoners wore vests with flannel sleeves. But the ones who held her attention longest were the elegant merchants with long coats and round hats.

"Finished," called Pita. "Am going." Lala scrambled down from the wall. For Pita to go without her was not to be thought of. With as much dignity as possible, she led the way. This time they stalked through the wagon shed and up the zaguán to the patio where the fountain water trickled.

Maman was resting in her room. She and Lala would eat there. Papá was entertaining scouts and merchants of the caravan. They would eat on the long, high table in the kitchen.

Maman looked at the embroidery. Pleased, she told

her small daughter: "You are improving with the colcha stitch."

Lala looked away, only to meet Nana's gaze, which seemed to pierce her like an arrow. Suddenly she did not feel hungry, but Nana stood by her plate.

"Eat," she said. Lala ate.

After what seemed an eternity of eating, it was siesta time. But not for Lala. On the floor by the window of her room, Pita was sitting. She was taking out the embroidery stitches that she had put in that morning. Lala would have liked to have told her, "If you had looked half the time, you would need to take out only half the stitches." She thought it wiser not to say it. When Pita had finished, Lala took the colcha and patiently put the stitches in again. Nana watched.

The company had finished dinner. They were singing American songs.

> *"I come from Alabama*
> *With my banjo on my knee.*
> *I'm going to Louisiana,*
> *My Susanna for to see."*

Lala listened, nodding her head to the rhythm of the music. Presently, still stitching, she joined the singing.

> *"I had a dream the other night*
> *When everything was still.*
> *I thought I saw Susanna*
> *A-coming down the hill."*

Lala looked around for Pita. The little Indian girl was asleep, still sitting on the floor beneath the window. Nana came over, looked at the embroidery, said, "Bueno," folded it and put it away. Lala danced around the room still singing the American song.

> *"O, Susanna! O, don't you cry for me,*
> *I've come from Alabama, with my banjo on*
> *my knee."*

It had been a wonderful, exciting day of adventure. A day to remember.

> *"O, Susanna! O, don't you cry for me."*

 *Chapter
Nine*

*Getting Ready for
the Saint's Day*

For a week all the women, who for most of the year were the hacienda spinners and dyers, had become sewing women. The cumbersome Spanish-colonial looms were pushed against the walls of the weaving room, and the women sang to their babies, cut cloth, and measured and basted and sewed it into fiesta dresses.

When the caravan came, the Patrón bought bolts of gay, bright calico cloth for new dresses for all the hacienda women, young girls and small girls and

111

babies. "Calico!" the women had exclaimed. "From the States!" they had said, fingering it. There were as many prints and colors as the freighters had brought with them. It had taken Maman many days to give out each piece, of the chosen color and design, and to estimate the length of cloth each dress would need. Now the women were making the dresses for the ball the Patrón would give for them on the evening of his name-day feast. The hacienda rang with laughter and song.

After much discussion, Carmen had been set the task of making the dresses that she, María, Rosa, and Lupe would wear. Carmen was pleased and not pleased. She liked to sew. She wanted to be with the women in the sewing room, but, on the other hand, she might miss something that might happen where María, Lupe, and Rosa worked with the Patrona. She went quickly, before the Patrona had a chance to change her mind, but as she went, she complained loudly and bitterly.

Nana's and Pita's fiesta dresses had been made in the States. Rita had sent them, explaining that they were proper, according to the fashions in Washington. Nana did not like them. Neither she nor Pita wore them. Instead they wore what they always wore,

112

skirts and blouses of handspun, hand-dyed wool, and cotton trimmed in handmade lace and flower embroidery. Secretly Maman was pleased. She was sorry about the calico, even though the Patrón and the women were pleased with it. As for the dresses from the States, she thought they were horrible.

The women in the sewing room sewed and sang. María, Lupe, and Rosa, under the supervision of the Patrona, whitewashed and scrubbed and polished and sang.

Lala and Pita were busy from sunrise to siesta every day. With Nana to help them, they had made new crepe-paper flowers for the altar in the chapel and for all the nichos in the walls where the wooden santos lived.

Then the santero came, an old man blessed with many years. Like a troubadour, he traveled the land and came only once a year to the hacienda of the Patrón. He always came before Saint John's Day to repair the santos, to make new ones if new ones were needed, and to paint the santos' wooden robes in the earth-colors that he made and carried with him. Lala and Pita thought themselves his most valuable assistants. He let them choose the colors for San Juan, San Antonio, San Martín and San José. They sewed

dresses of lace and silk for the little wooden figures of Santa María, la Virgen de Guadalupe, and Santa Ana. The santero knew the Saints much better than he knew the people of the towns and haciendas where he worked. The Saints were dear to him. They were his compadres, his companions, the friends of his heart. He told the two young helpers all he knew about them.

All the days were busy days and happy days. All the people worked. Even old blind Juana helped the candlemaker dip the candles. As for the troubadour, his sickness left him, and new songs swarmed his heart like honey bees swarming a new hive. Time seemed to run swiftly.

At last the panes of Pittsburgh glass were tight and unbroken in the sala windows. It had taken all of them to get the glass in properly. The Patrón and Luis had supervised. The cabinetmaker had done the work. José and Tranquilino and even Pedro the water boy and Rafael the bell ringer had given advice. And now, at last, the panes were in. María said that she, and she alone, could wash them properly. They shone with her polishing. Everyone looked at them and through them. "Pittsburgh glass," Pedro told Rafael. "Sí," Rafael answered. "From the States."

The ceiling vigas in the sala had been newly painted with earth colors. The earth floor had been saturated with ox blood, and Lupe and Rosa had polished it, using small, smooth polishing stones. Chacho came in with the new Brussels carpet, unrolled it from its wrappings, and spread it carefully on the sala floor. Everyone exclaimed at the beauty of its design and the perfection of its weave. No one walked on it!

Maman looked with pride at her sala. The walls had been freshly whitewashed and the wainscot, baby-high, painted with terro de oro. Around the walls ran bench seats made of adobe and covered with Indian woven blankets washed only yesterday with pounded yucca roots. On the walls were many mirrors and many candle sconces. The crystal prisms from the candelabra reflected candlelight in tiny, quivering rainbows. There were only two pieces of furniture, a ceiling-high, carved trastero and a high, carved table. Both were of walnut, and both were polished to perfection.

The Patrona was satisfied. The chapel was in order. The altar linens had been laundered. All the sleeping rooms had been cleaned. All the patios' floors had been scrubbed and all the vigas wiped with

116

dampened cloth. The flower beds had been weeded. Her house was in readiness for the day the guests would arrive.

Now for the preparation of the food. There would be at least a hundred people to feed—not just to feed but to feast. This was no ordinary fiesta, but the name day of the hacienda Patrón.

José dragged in a heavy, high-backed chair. As on a throne, the Patrona would sit here, in the center of her kitchen, to supervise, direct, examine, and taste the foods that would be prepared.

Workmen came, carrying the meats, venison, bear, buffalo humps, beef, and mutton. Lupe and Rosa plucked the chickens. Chacho brought sackloads of beans, corn and squash, onions and chili.

Although the Patrona sat on the throne, María was queen of the kitchen. Her word was law. She shouted at Rosa and Lupe to hurry, hurry, hurry, plucking the chickens. She needed them not tomorrow but now. She was everywhere at once, as quick as if she had been half the size she was. She baked and roasted and fried and boiled.

First came the sweets: wheat-flour pan dulce, sweet cakes stuffed with dried fruits, fried pies stuffed with mincemeat, cookies flavored with aniseed, bread

117

pudding with raisin and wine sauce, flan with burned sugar, custard thick with fruit.

The meats were made ready for roasting and boiling. The fat short tamales were wrapped in cornhusks. Goats' cheese was made and flavored with chili. Corn was ground, boiled, mashed, and roasted for the different corn dishes. Beans were boiled slowly, and rice brought in from the storeroom. Tacos and tortillas would be prepared as they were needed. Great amounts would be needed. Guests would stay ten days at the least, and perhaps a week more.

Hacienda men, except the vaqueros, went with Luis to build luminarias of piñon wood: two sticks crossed with two sticks, building upward into little wood towers. When they were fired, they would light the way for all the coaches and carriages and carretas from the outer gates through the big doors into the zaguán.

This done, they made the faroletas, small sacks half full of sand, holding fat little candles. These would make a lighted crown on the rooftop of the trading post, the storehouse, the mill, and the hacienda. They would be placed at intervals on all the high adobe walls. On the eve and the night of fiesta the hacienda lights in the rolling foothills of the Sangre de Cristo Mountains would outshine the stars in the canopy of sky above the lonely land.

At last, everything was ready. Everything was waiting. Even the adobe bricks in the outer walls seemed to glow with warm and friendly welcome. Luis and Chacho were posted at the outer gates. María sat by the double doors of the zaguán, holding the great key in her hands, ready to turn it in its lock. The workers stood in two long rows from the doors by the sala to the doors opening to the wagon shed. Dressed in their best, they, too, were ready and waiting.

The vaqueros would take care of the horses and mules, the coaches and carriages and the carretas. Other men would carry the leather trunks and the rawhide chests of the guests to the waiting rooms. The women would conduct each load of passengers warmly, gayly from the sala, where they first would go, to the many patios that had been made ready for them.

The Patrón, the Patrona, and Lala would give the embrace of welcome to each guest entering the zaguán. Maman and Lala wore their dresses from Paris. They were alike in color, in make, in size: of

119

blue velvet, full-skirted, small-waisted. Their printed slippers were also of velvet, blue like the dresses.

The guests began to arrive. First came the Padre from Taos and the six altar boys he would need to assist him at vespers, at Mass, at the blessing of the bonfires, the hacienda, and its people, and the baptism of new hacienda babies.

Then came the coaches and carriages, the carretas, and the young men on horseback. Godfathers and godmothers came with their families, their relatives, their servants. Great-aunts and great-uncles, cousins, second cousins, third cousins came. They came from Taos and Mora and Las Vegas. They came from Albuquerque and Santa Fe. Hunters and trappers, traders and scouts, officials of government—all with their families, all with their servants—came for fiesta, came for a fortnight.

Now was the Eve of Saint John's Day. Guests had been arriving since midday. Quantities of food had been served. There had been talk and laughter. But until the sunset hour there had been no festival activities.

With the setting of the sun, when the hills and the mountains of the Sangre de Cristo were as red as the blood of Christ, whence they received their name, fiesta began.

120

It began with the firing of guns, many guns, a salute from the hacienda workers to the hacienda Patrón. The candles were lit and the luminarias and the faroletas. The small chapel bell was rung. The Padre came, in the vestment of vespers, attended by his altar boys in snow-white surplices, carrying candles in candlesticks of gold. The little chapel and the patio outside it and the archway of the zaguán were filled with people kneeling for evensong. The fragrance of flowers mingled with the musty scent of incense and the tallow drip from the candles. The songs of the people rose upward, to be lost in the stillness of night. Supper was served in the sala, in the kitchen, in the patios, and in the houses of the workers.

Afterward, the Patrón asked the Patrona if for his feast day she would sing his favorite song. This was a song that the Patrona's French mother from Louisiana had sung to her French-Canadian trapper husband in New Orleans and in Taos many years before. When the Patrona sang it, she always wondered if her Spanish husband really liked it or if it was his way of saying, "My favorite because you sing it."

Laughing, she stood before him, small, beautiful, French in every heartbeat but true to the traditions of Spain because her husband was Spanish. She had no musical accompaniment. She needed none. Clear and resounding her voice filled the sala and the zaguán.

> *"Alouette, gentille alouette,*
> *Alouette, je te plumerai*
> *Alouette, alouette, Ah!"*

At the far end of the zaguán the troubadour's voice could be heard. Lala clapped her hands with joy. He was coming to sing for them. He was bringing to Papá's fiesta the songs that had swarmed his heart like honey bees wanting a new hive. Everyone waited, listening. Ah! he was singing "La Paloma," beloved song of Spanish people. At first he sang alone, walking slowly up the zaguán, strumming his guitar.

> *"Ay, chinita, que sí!*
> *Ay, que dame tu amor."*

One by one, other voices joined him. At first these were only the men's voices.

> *"Ay, que vente conmigo, chinita,*
> *A donde vivo yo."*

Gradually the women began singing as they walked with their men in the candle-lit shadows of the wide zaguán.

> *"Ay, chinita, que sí!*
> *Ay, que dame tu amor."*

By the time the strollers reached the sala, all were singing, old and young, Spanish, Indian, and French.

> *"Ay, que vente conmigo, chinita,*
> *A donde vivo yo."*

They sang the night away. Even the Padre joined them, his people, his spiritual children, blessing them as he sang with them.

> *"Ay, chinita, que sí!*
> *Ay, que dame tu amor."*

 *Chapter*
Ten

Fiesta of San Juan

With the first pink glow upon the eastern sky herald-
ing the rising sun, the second gunfire salute was
given by the hacienda workmen, accompanied by
the popping of giant firecrackers by all the hacienda
boys too young to own a gun. The long-planned-for
day had come. This was the Feast of John the Baptist
and the feast day also for all whose names were Juan
or Juana, or Joan or John. This was for some a birthday as well as a name day, but not for the Patrón or
for his son. They bore the proud name because it had
been handed down to them through generations of
first sons to first sons.

Jean-Baptiste was also at that time Canada's patron saint, and, therefore, to all the Spanish festivities the Patrona had gayly added French-Canadian ones. She remembered that her mother had been careful to add the traditions of Quebec to the ones she had been heir to in French New Orleans. Now no one in the hacienda remembered or cared which traditions had come from French Louisiana, which from French Quebec, and which from Old World or New World Spain.

Immediately after the sunrise salute, the Patrona gathered together all the ladies who were guests, all their little girls, and the serving women they had brought with them, and all the hacienda women, their little girls, and the women relatives who had come to visit. They went to the mountain river to bathe and swim in the first hour of sunrise.

At a certain place on the riverbank where old cottonwood trees bent their leafy branches protectingly over the water, the worker women swam: first the elder, then the young girls. Farther downstream, where huge boulders cupped a pool of dark green water, the Patrona and her guests swam in the ice-cold river. They followed the same pattern, first those who were older and then the young. This was not done in sporting play. It was not done for fun. It was

126

a rite. The old tradition promised that the women who bathed in the running waters of a mountain river on the Fiesta of San Juan would enjoy a year of health and happiness. The Day of San Juan comes in June, when the peaks of the Sangre de Cristos are still snow-crested and the river waters carry the melting ice of winter's ice-bound canyons. In June, morning at sunrise still carries the chill of night.

After the first numbing plunge into the icy water, Lala enjoyed the swimming. She loved the Río. She liked to stand on its banks in late springtime when the flood waters of melting snow and waterfalls that had been turned to stilled ribbons of ice swept boulders and uprooted trees and great bites of river-bank along in their torrent. She liked to come here to the river on a lazy midsummer day when the river-banks were covered in wild flowers blooming, and birds nested and sang in the cottonwood and the willow. She liked to come in autumn when the cottonwood trees were crowned with golden leaves and the ground was carpeted with the crimson and russet and bronze of ground oak and kinnikinnick. She liked the Río in winter when the whole world was white with snow and the water was encased in crystal.

But no. She corrected her dreaming. She liked it

127

best now on the Day of San Juan when she and her cousins were swimming and splashing and ducking each other in the depths of the still, green pool. A big trout lived here in the shade of the boulder. She had seen it. She wondered where it hid on the morning of the feast day.

Much too soon, the little girls thought, Lala's mother said that swim time had ended. But returning to the hacienda was also fun. On this day, going to and from the river, Lala could forget about being the small Patrona of a big hacienda. She ran, jumped, hopped, leaped, and shouted with the other girls. She outruns, outshouts all of them, the Patrona thought, watching her small daughter. My poor little one, everything she does, she does with all her heart. Many times she will need to hurt it. But now Lala's heart knew only the joy of being alive on a gay June morning. She taught the others how to play the stick game. She had watched Indian boys play it. She knew how it was done. She liked teaching the girls to play a boy's game.

It was only after they came inside the hacienda walls again that the different groups separated, each group going on in its own pattern, which the custom of the times had made. The children of the workers went to the houses of the hacienda workers, taking their relatives and friends with them. There they put on their fiesta dresses and their best rebozos and walked in family groups up the zaguán to hear fiesta Mass.

Lala and her cousins went into the patios where their sleeping rooms were, to take off the wide skirts and cotton blouses and blue rebozos and put on the tight-fitting, full-skirted silks and satins and lace mantillas that they would wear to Mass. They, too, walked sedately with their parents up the zaguán to the crowded chapel.

The Padre led the procession, flanked by the altar boys carrying lighted homemade candles in golden candlesticks. After them came Luis, swinging the incense burner. Then came the Patrón, his wife, and his daughter. The troubadour, playing his violin, led the choir of hacienda singers that he and the Patrona had trained. Others also played the violin and strummed the guitar, and other groups sang, not necessarily the same tunes or the same songs, but all with fervor and enjoyment.

The Padre led the people in solemn, singing procession to the kitchen and storerooms, to the patio rooms and the workrooms, and to the little houses, blessing them. They went to the corrals, and the Padre blessed the horses. This was the little foal's first blessing.

Lala shyly, secretly blew a small kiss in its direction. The Padre blessed the sheep flock, which on this day would not be taken to graze on the foothills. The Padre blessed the fields and the fruit trees. He could come only once a year. He measured his parish in hundreds of miles and had many places to visit. But when he came, he wanted to make certain that the Hand of God rested lovingly on the people, and on their possessions, on their work and their food supply.

They returned to the chapel, still in solemn procession, and the zaguán smelled pleasantly of gunpowder and incense, of melted candle tallow, and of food slowly cooking in the kitchen and the kitchen patio. Lala sniffed. She was hungry. She was very hungry!

Above the chapel door, the big bell and the little bell were ringing, proclaiming the feast day of the Patrón and of his patron saint. The Mass was a High Mass, the altar boys served at it, the hacienda choir sang it. The chapel was filled to its open doors, and the people knelt also in the patio by the fountain and out into the zaguán.

After Mass, the Padre baptized all the little Juans and Juanas who would claim this day as their name day. The Patrón and the Patrona and Lala, and Baptiste in name because he was not present, were the godfathers and godmothers. This meant that until death there would be a spiritual bond between them and the babies they held in their arms.

At last there was breakfast, gay, heavy, and long-lasting. After breakfast, all the Juans and Juanas and Jean-Baptistes of other years came into the sala to exchange small gifts and felicitations with their Patrón and to make the pretty speeches their mothers had taught them. The Patrón knew them all and had some special word of praise for each of them. Maman and Lala sat stiffly on chairs used for this occasion, but Papá stood, courteously, kindly, fatherly, giving each his moment of importance. Carmen came, leading old blind Juana, and the Patrón bent to kiss her withered cheeks. Lala felt tears of pride making little rivers of salt on her face, and looking at her mother, she saw that tears glistened in Maman's eyes. She touched her mother's hand, and her mother took it, holding it lovingly.

The knocker on the great door near the sala was hammered, once, loud, demanding. In the same breath the big bell in the chapel began to peal. This was no joyous ringing. This was the clanging of fear. "Indios, Indios!" A whispering wind blowing through the sala, into the patios, the length of the zaguán. "Indios, Indios!"

Silently, swiftly the people fled—the women and

131

children to hide, the men to arm. Only the Patrón, the Patrona, and Lala, with Nana standing behind them, were left in the sala. María, at her usual place at the door, stood rooted in fear, peeking out the panel peekhole. Luis came running into the sala.

"Who knocks?" the Patrón asked.

"Canuto," María whispered. Then, realizing her Patrón was near, she cried out fiercely, "It's that Canuto, and he has three warriors with him."

The Patrón said to Luis, "Find out why he comes."

Returning, Luis said, "He brings gifts for your feast day. That is what he says."

"And will expect a gift in return, I suppose." The Patrón was irritated.

Luis shrugged. "That is the custom of his tribe," he answered.

The Patrón laughed shortly. "Well, he cannot have the gift he wants. It will have to be another horse. Find Chacho and tell him to bring the chestnut, not the mare. The young horse."

Luis went to find Chacho. María unlocked the door.

Chief Canuto, followed by three of his warriors, entered. They wore moccasins, loincloths, headbands —nothing else. Lala looked quickly. Neither their

132

faces nor their bodies were painted. They came in peace.

The Patrona told María, "Find Lupe and Rosa. Prepare three sacks of food for the Chief's warriors."

María pretended not to hear her.

"María." The Patrona spoke firmly.

María decided that she had to get the food, though she disapproved of feeding "wild Indians." Fully recovered from her fright, she said in Apache as she passed Canuto: "Why don't you wear clothes?"

Canuto understood Apache, but made no sign that he had heard her. The Patrón understood. He hid his smile.

Canuto talked with the Patrón of many things. He spoke in Spanish. He said that beaver were getting scarce, that the buffalo were almost gone, that his braves had been at peace for many days. The Patrón listened and gave the expected answers. He knew that no Indian comes immediately to the reason for a visit. Such a thing is not to be thought of.

Finally, Canuto beckoned his warriors. "Gifts for your day of feasting," he said. Each warrior unrolled his bundle: beaver pelts, tanned deerskin, a buffalo robe.

The Patrón praised the gifts and thanked the giver.

133

He motioned Chacho to bring the chestnut. "I, too, have a gift for you," he told Canuto.

Canuto praised the gift and thanked the giver. María, Lupe, and Rosa came in with the sacks of food and put them on the floor by the Patrona. Their manner said that if their Patrona told them to bring food, they would bring it. But they would bring it to the Patrona and not to the "wild Indians." Neither the warriors nor the Patrona looked at the food, but they knew it was there.

After a silence, Canuto spoke again. "The Appaloosa foal," he said. "You do not sell it?"

"No," the Patrón answered, "nor have it stolen."

There was another silence. Then Canuto said, "This being your day, you will race me, perhaps. Two of my best ponies against the foal."

The Patrón shook his head. "The foal is not for betting."

"And not a gift, not to be given?" asked Canuto.

The Patrón hesitated, "As a gift, perhaps, but only to one of my blood."

Lala gave a little gasp. Papá was going to give her the foal! It was to be hers. She was to own a horse. Her face lighted with joy and her black eyes sparkled. At her gasp, Canuto turned to look at her. For a

134

heartbeat, their glances met. One cold, appraising; the other warm with joy. Both fearless.

Lightly Canuto leaped upon the horse that had been given him. Even without a bridle, he rode superbly. Looking over his shoulders, he said, "For almost a moon my braves have been peaceful." The warriors picked up the sacks of food and followed their Chief. Luis locked the double doors of the zaguán.

After a short silence, the Patrona said, "Nana, tell Rafael to ring the little chapel bell. Since this is a day for rejoicing, we will continue to rejoice." The Patrón held out his hand to his two dear ones, and with dignity and pride they went to the sala of the fountain to give hospitality and entertainment to their guests in proper and fitting manner.

The daylight festivities for the Day of San Juan were mostly for the men. In the plaza before the trading post there was horse racing, cock fighting, and what was called a rooster pull. There is always a rooster pull on Saint John's Day. The men, riding horseback, separate into teams. Riders of each team try to take the rooster from the other team. It is a rough game, requiring skilled riders to play it.

The ladies did not attend these boisterous activities

135

but stayed in the patios, chatting. The men returned for dinner, but not for siesta or merienda. After the late evening supper, the important festivities began. Everyone attended. The vaqueros took turns, and the sheepherders came and the old and the sick.

Three bonfires had been built in the plaza before the trading post. The people stood around in little groups, waiting for the Patrón to light the fires and for the Padre to bless them. Three lines of small girls, singing, came through the doors of the zaguán. They were dressed in their new fiesta dresses. Their black braids were intertwined with colored yarns. Their rebozos were thrown lightly across their shoulders. They danced and sang around the lighted bonfires. Flames shooting upward, red, yellow, orange, lighted the faces of the little dancers and intensified the vivid colors of the calico dresses. Lala was very proud of the little girls. She and the troubadour had taught them their songs, and she and her mother had taught them the dancing steps. When the dance was completed, the little girls ran to their families to be kissed and praised for their performance.

Again there was a procession led by the Padre around the walls of the plaza of the post. This was a

gay procession with lively songs and violins and guitars and two accordions. The men fired their guns; the boys popped their giant firecrackers; the women and the girls carried lighted candles. At the end of the procession, in a small carreta pulled by a reluctant burro, María's youngest grandson rode, struggling with a young lamb which was supposed to lie quietly in his arms but did not. The boy represented Saint John, and because of this, or perhaps because he was her favorite grandson, María would allow no one but herself to lead, pull, and prod the lazy burro.

After the procession, the balls began. There were two of them, one in the warehouse by the post, the other in the weaving room inside the hacienda. Both rooms were bare of furniture, festooned with paper streamers and paper flowers, and with a plank platform at one end for the musicians. The ball for the workers was in the warehouse; for the guests, in the weaving room. But the musicians went back and forth between the two, each group wanting to play for the Patrón. The Americans also went back and forth, wanting to see everything.

The outer gates in the walls were closed, but the doors leading into the zaguán were left open. Outside, the bonfires and the luminarias and the faroletas glowed, sputtered, burned out, and were relit. Inside, the sala, the zaguán, the patios, and the rooms were lighted by hundreds of candles. The stars hung low and the moon was bright. "Everything to light the night of Papá's feast day," Lala thought happily.

For the night festivities, Lala and her mother looked completely Spanish. They wore Spanish dresses, black, scarlet, and gold, with black lace mantillas and high tortoise-shell combs. Their slippers were scarlet, and their long-fringed silk shawls from China were richly embroidered. Their earrings, necklaces, bracelets, and rings were of gold filegree. Papá was very proud. "Two Spanish beauties," he said so low that only they could hear.

The Patrón and the Patrona led the promenade. Lala was partnered by her favorite uncle, who had come from Mora for the occasion. He was French and had always delighted her with his stories of the old days when New Spain had been truly a newfound land. Both he and his father had trapped for beaver for the Hudson's Bay Company of Canada. He used to recite Habitant poetry by the hour to Lala and Baptiste.

This memory brought thoughts of her brother. Last year he had been her partner in the dancing.

She missed him tonight. She wished he were here to see the foal when Papá gave it to her. He would give it to her, she was almost sure. He had almost said that was what he was going to do. The Indians would not steal it. Papá had told Canuto that they would not be able to steal it. Still, she wished Baptiste were here. Smiling, she looked up at her uncle. He must enjoy this night of celebration.

After the promenade, dancing began, the two-step, the polka, the waltz, the schottische, all the dances that were dear to their hearts. Interspersed with the dancing were many songs: Spanish, Mexican, French, Habitant, all the songs that were dear to the people's hearts. The Americans sang in English:

> *"Oh, say, were you ever on the Rio Grand?*
> *Way you river!*
> *Oh, were you ever on that strand,*
> *For we're bound to the Rio Grand."*

Lala loved the American songs. True, as her mother said, some of them were boisterous, but to Lala they were strong and hearty. She tried to find the word that described them: new. Yes. They sounded new. New and strong.

140

Long after Nana had come for her and she had gone to bed, she could hear them singing:

> *"And away you Rio!*
> *Way you Rio!*
> *Sing fare you well,*
> *My pretty young girls.*
> *For we're bound to the Rio Grand."*

 **Chapter Eleven**

Visitors and Strangers

Lala wiggled about, trying to find a comfortable spot in the hole-in-the-wall and yet see out into the plaza by the trading post. She had been here such a long time this morning, but she had not yet seen what she was looking for. She knew that Pita, hiding in her usual place at the foot of the wall, was miserable.

Poor Pita, Lala thought. She really wants to be good all the time. What a sorrow I must be to her.

She wiggled backwards out of the hole to look down at Pita, who was watching the trail on the far bank of the river. Lala crawled into the hole again.

I will watch just a little longer, she promised herself. Just long enough to think about all the things that have happened this week. If she has not come by then, I won't look any more. I will go back to the house.

But she wanted to see the little girl again. She had seen her yesterday and the day before. Tante Rita said that the immigrant wagons would be moving on again surely by sunrise tomorrow. "Little girl, I want so very much to see you once more," Lala called softly down into the plaza. No one heard her call. The plaza was full of milling people, freighters, Indians, hunters, trappers, scouts, immigrants, and a handful of American soldiers. But no little girl. Lala settled herself to wait.

True to the promise she had made she began naming over the events of the week before. Papá's fiesta had long been over and all the guests had gone, leaving, in the place of the laughter and merriment that they had brought, great pools of emptiness and silence.

The reason for each day, it seemed to Lala, was her visit to the foal. In wonderment, she watched it grow, week by week, and watched it getting to know her.

Then Tante Rita and Tío Toto had come. Though

144

the hacienda people had known they were coming and had expected them, their actual arrival had caused great excitement. They came in a United States Army ambulance because they could travel in it more quickly than by heavy, cumbersome coach. They had been accompanied by Outriders. Outriders of the United States of America! Lala was impressed. She could not forgive herself for not having been in the secret place to watch their arrival.

But nothing could dim the excitement and joy of their coming. All the workers were as delighted as the Patrona and Lala. Doña Rita, they called Tante Rita; Don Miguel was their name for Tío Toto. They kept exclaiming, "Doña Rita, you are here!" "Don Miguel, you have come." It was as gay a time as Papá's fiesta had been.

Tante Rita and Tío Toto had brought presents for everyone. No one was forgotten, not even the newest babies, or the troubadour, who was not supposed to have stayed so long. Lala said, "This is like Christmas, Tante Rita. Just like Christmas, Tío Toto, only better because it is extra." It was as exciting to look at the other presents as it was to look at one's own. Everyone said, "From the States! From the Washington of the Americans!"

Besides presents to wear and to use, Tante Rita had brought new kinds of foods. She taught María how to make potato salad. María was shocked. "No way to eat potatoes," she said. "Food like this could kill the liver." The others who tasted the potato salad were inclined to agree with María. It was not proper to prepare potatoes in such a way, and also everyone knew that rice and beans were better than potatoes. Doña Rita showed María how to cook oatmeal. It was to be eaten for the morning meal with milk. Milk! Milk was to be boiled with coffee, not eaten from a dish!

Tío Toto had brought Papá an ice-cream freezer. He showed him how to freeze the custard María made. The ice cream was a grand success. Everyone liked it. Pedro, Rafael, José, and even Tranquilino wanted to turn the freezer, but María would permit no one but herself or the Patrón to turn it.

"We will build a larger icehouse on the Río," the Patrón promised, "and cut much ice next winter. Everyone can have ice cream every day."

"Ice cream everyday!" Lala said. "That will be even better than an extra Christmas."

Besides new kinds of food, Tante Rita had brought new fashions. She showed her sister how to twist her hair in a chignon.

"It's simple," she told Maman. "The American ladies do their own hair."

"And Monsieur Adrian? If you could do your own hair, what did he do?" Maman asked.

Rita laughed. "For one month I had him stand by my chair to translate to me what was being said in English. Now I understand and speak it well." Rita let her eyes, her hands, her shoulders help her express her pride in the way she had learned English.

Maman looked at her sister and replied in English, "How nice that you could learn."

Rita kissed her sister lightly. She had always loved to tease her.

Tante Rita and Tío Toto had brought new ideas, too. The new ideas were shared only with Papá and Maman, but Lala listened. Tante did most of the talking, but anyone could see that Tío Toto agreed with what she said. "The United States is wonderful. Such a new nation, so strong, so vital. Not yet a century in age, and it reaches from ocean to ocean." Rita looked around. They were listening. She continued. "The Americans are not subject to a king or an emperor. They are their government. They have a voice in government. They have a responsibility in government. Their flag is not a royal banner handed down to the people by the families of royalty. Their flag is

147

a symbol of what those who founded the nation believed the people who lived after them would live by."

Lala remembered everything that Tante Rita said. She had never thought about belonging to a country and having a flag that was a standard to live by. She could remember only the flag of Mexico, and although it had flown from public buildings in Santa Fe, the Spaniards of New Spain had neither loved nor accepted it.

Her thoughts were interrupted by a worried cry from Pita. "Señorita Lala, Doña Rita is on the far riverbank. She crosses the river now."

If Tante Rita had reached the river, there was need to leave the hole-in-the-wall at once, before Chacho discovered her, Lala knew. She would never have been able to slip away yesterday, or the day before, or today if Tante had not wanted to ride beyond the river and take Chacho with her as her groom boy. Quickly Lala slid down the wall. When there was need to run, she was as swift-footed as Pita. The two girls ran fast and close to the long, windowless wall of the hacienda and in through the gates of the wagon shed. Long before the riders had reached the corral, the girls were walking up the cobblestoned zaguán.

148

The workers they met gave the day's greeting, and Lala smiled in return. Pita covered her face with her rebozo. Only her enormous eyes could be seen: worried eyes, frightened and guilty. No one noticed them. The people they met noticed only Lala's happy smile.

The Patrona was busy with María in the kitchen patio. Since her sister had ceased to believe in hacienda walls and the work pattern of hacienda living, she had not asked her to assist in the teaching, supervising, and care of the hacienda people.

The Patrona wondered if perhaps her sister was not right in her thinking. Perhaps living in one of the newly established towns would be better for everyone. Safer, too, now that the Americans had promised to control the Indians. Maman thought worriedly of Canuto. Would he ever come to know that this vast land was large enough for all of them?

Lala waved at her mother as she passed the kitchen patio. The Patrona, busy with her thoughts, did not look up, did not ask her daughter where she had been. Taking Pita and the still unfinished colcha with her, Lala went into her aunt's patio to wait for her.

When her aunt came in, Lala said "Did you have a pleasant ride this morning, Tante?"

149

Her aunt nodded, "Yes. And you? How have you spent the hours since breakfast?"

Lala did not answer, but lifted her embroidery for her aunt to see.

"You sew a fine stitch," her aunt complimented her.

There was a small silence. Lala did not know how to say what she felt she must say. She must be very careful not to let Tante Rita know that she had seen the immigrant girl, watched her playing. Finally she said, "When you came, you told us that you had passed some immigrant wagons on the trail. Tell me about them."

"Yes. We camped one night near them. What do you want to know about them?"

Lala began to embroider. "Oh, everything."

Her aunt laughed. "Immigrants are fine people. They start out from their old homes, hoping to find new homes and a better way of life for their children."

"Oh," Lala looked up, "they have children?"

"Of course they have children."

"Little girls?"

"Yes," her aunt said, thinking back. "There was one very pretty little girl. She looked about eight

150

years old, about two years younger than you, I should think."

Lala corrected her. "The day after tomorrow, on Saint Anne's Day, I will be entering my eleventh year. That would make her three years younger."

Her aunt shook her head. "No. Not the way the Americans figure ages and birthdays. The Americans figure that when you are ten years old, you are ten years until your eleventh birthday. The Spanish say that after your tenth birthday you are in your eleventh year. That would make you about two years older than the little girl I saw."

Lala was not interested in the way birthdays were figured. She wanted to know about the little girl. "Did this little girl have her hair in braids as yellow as sunflowers? Did she have eyes as blue as Blanca's? Was she pretending that the corncob she carried was a doll?" she asked.

Her aunt looked at her. Bees buzzed in the flower beds. María was singing in the kitchen. Somewhere a baby cried.

Lala realized what she had said. Now her aunt knew that she had seen the little girl with yellow braids and the eyes as blue as Blanca's. Her heart seemed to have jumped into her throat, filling it so that she could not speak. Pita gave a little whimpering moan, and Lala looked at her.

Pita had known all the time that some day somebody would find out that they climbed the wall and looked through the hole by the wheel. Lala corrected her thinking: not they, only she would be found out. Pita had not wanted to go. Pita was not to be punished. She looked at her aunt. "I saw the little girl," she said. "No one else but me." She closed her eyes and waited for the world to fall apart.

Her aunt laughed. Lala opened her eyes in surprise. "So you know the secret place," her aunt spoke lightly.

Lala was horrified. "I did not tell you. No one told you," she said fiercely.

Her aunt laughed again. "My dear, every young person for the last two hundred years has known and used the hole-in-the-wall by the old mill wheel."

"Did you know about it?"

"Of course."

"Did Maman know?"

"Perhaps."

Lala gave Pita a teasing smile. "Did Nana know?"

Tante Rita also turned a teasing smile on Pita. "Nana knew, but she never looked."

Laughter filled the patio: Tante's, Lala's, and even Pita's. Tranquilino, looking in, told Pedro: "Doña Rita and the señorita Lala are as alike as two peas in a pod."

Tante was serious again. "What do you want to know about Little Yellow Braids?" she asked gently. Lala was very dear to her, and she wanted her to experience all that life might hold.

Lala hesitated. At last she said, "She had a corncob that she pretended was her doll. She was singing to it. I . . . I want to send Chacho with one of my dolls for her." Seeing a flash of disapproval on her aunt's face, she added quickly, "I have not played with dolls since I was eight years old, but the little girl needs one. It seems she does not own one."

Her aunt said, "Come here, Annette, I want to talk with you. If you want to give the little girl a doll, that is good. But sending it to her by your groom boy is not good. You are not a princess, little one, you are an American. If you have a gift for the child, you will take it to her."

Lala was confused. She knew she was not a princess. A princess was of royal blood in France or Spain.

Seeing the confusion on Lala's face, the aunt tried to explain what she meant. It was difficult to put in

153

words. "When the nation was founded, it was upon the belief that all men must be free and equal."

Lala's confusion deepened. Tante tried again. "Being free means freedom from slavery. It also means freedom from want and from fear. Do you understand this, Annette?"

Lala nodded. She understood freedom.

Her aunt continued, "Being equal is more difficult to understand. It does not mean, necessarily, to have equal possessions or perhaps abilities or even desires. It means that every American has the right to have equal opportunity to reach the full measure of his worth. It means that every American has the responsibility to make those rights possible for all Americans, within his power to do so."

There was a silence. Then Tante asked, "Do you understand, Annette?"

"I think I do, Tante Rita. I am trying to understand."

Her aunt hugged her. "Good. Try to understand, because the flag is the symbol of this belief. If you accept the country and the flag, you must accept all those things for which it stands."

Lala went back to the problem of giving the doll. "I cannot give her the doll. I am not permitted to go

154

in the public plaza, only on feast days when no one but guests are present."

Doña Rita laughed. "You will be permitted this time. A half hour before sundown, come here with your doll. You and I will go. Not Pita. Not Nana. Not Chacho. Just you and I, two Norte Americanos."

But the Patrón, the Patrona, and Tío Toto decided that they must go with the two overly brave "Americans." Looking at them, Doña Rita shrugged. It would have been better for the two children to meet alone. This meeting was important. It was important to Lala, the young girl. It was important to the woman she would become. She said, aside, to Lala, "Something is better than nothing." Lala laughed. This was an old Spanish saying. All the hacienda people used it when they wanted to express displeased acceptance.

María grudgingly unlocked the small door in the panel of the larger one, scowling her disapproval. The four grownups and the young girl walked across the plaza to where the immigrants were camped, their oxen safe in the corral of covered wagons surrounding them.

Doña Rita had a word for each.

Lala is like her, Maman thought. The entire world is her friend.

Almost at once, Doña Rita saw the woman whose little girl had talked with her when they had night-camped together on the trail. The woman, tall, thin, tired-looking, was putting sourdough biscuit in the Dutch oven over the coals of the supper fire. She remembered the beautiful lady from Washington and was glad to see her.

Tante explained that her niece, Annette, had a gift for her little daughter, and the woman said that her girl was toting water from the creek but that she would go to fetch her. They returned very quickly.

"This is Susan," the woman said.

"Susan?" Lala cried in delight. "Susanna!" The little girl hid in her mother's skirts, peeking out at Lala. Lala began singing, softly, softly:

> *"O, Susanna! O, don't you cry for me,*
> *I come from Alabama, with my banjo on my*
> *knee."*

Shyly, little Susan walked nearer, step by step. Lala held out the doll for her. "This is for you, Susanna." Slowly Susan took it, held it, looked down at it. As long as Lala lived, she would never forget the look that lighted the thin white face, or the tender way the little girl held the doll.

The first notes of taps were sounded by a bugler boy in uniform. Everything stopped: all the milling around, all the shouting, all the noise, all the disorder of a gathering place for many kinds of people. All eyes turned to the tower by the outer gates.

Slowly the great, beautiful flag of the United States of America billowed and furled against the reddening sky of sunset. Sweetly the notes of the bugle cut through the thin air of evening.

> *"Day is done . . ."*

The flag, drawn downward, swelled and folded and swelled against the crimson backdrop of departing day.

> *"Gone the sun . . .*
> *From the lake, from the hills, from the*
> *sky . . ."*

Lala stood transfixed. Suddenly she threw herself in her father's arms. "Papá. Papá. It is my flag. I have a flag. I have a country." She began to sob.

> *"All is well*
> *Safely rest . . ."*

157

Canuto, standing in the shadows of the covered wagons, watched Lala, watched the little girl with the yellow braids.

"God is nigh."

The flag had been taken down. Taps had been sounded. Day was done.

 ## Chapter
Twelve

Saint Anne's Day

The big iron key turned heavily in its lock, the carved door on its heavy iron hinges swung slowly inward. Lala sat up in bed, completely awake. This was not sunrise, her usual time of waking. This was the hour before dawn, when all the shadows of the night seemed to gather, reluctant to lose their moment of importance, reluctant to be dispelled by the brilliant light of the rising sun.

Nana entered, with Tante Rita following close behind. Nana was cross. She was outraged that Doña Rita had insisted upon breaking the pattern of day's beginning.

161

Tante Rita was conspiratorial, hushing Nana's complaints and Lala's questioning. "Hush. Do not waken your parents," she whispered. "Wrap this serape around you. Walk softly. Be very quiet."

She blew a kiss at Nana and patted her wrinkled cheek. Nana refused to smile. She disapproved of such a silly undertaking.

Tante Rita, holding Lala's hand, slipped through the patio and down the zaguán to the great doors near the sala, two dark shadows cutting through the gray ones. Tante Rita found the key to the little door, slipped outside, and pulled Lala after her. "Look," she whispered. "Look."

The immigrant train was moving through the gates the guard had opened for them. The great oxen lurched and pulled. The covered wagons creaked and swayed. By the side of each yoke of oxen walked a dark figure, prodding the beasts onward. No one else was to be seen. The immigrant train looked unreal, unearthly in the brooding light of pre-dawn. It looked lonely. The last wagon lumbered through the gates, which were instantly barred and would not be opened again until an hour after sunrise.

Lala felt a moment of desolation. "She has gone," she said sadly.

"I thought we might be able to catch a glimpse of Little Yellow Braids. That is why I brought you out here," her aunt said. "They have so little, except courage. America is built upon courage, Lala."

Lala looked at her in surprise. Her aunt, usually so lighthearted, seemed sad.

Lala too felt sad this morning. "I liked the little girl," she said, remembering the look Susanna had given the doll as she held it in her arms. Her aunt did not reply.

They went back silently to Lala's room. The fire in the fireplace was burning brightly. Nana had hot chocolate for them to drink. For a while they sipped the sweet, thick, frothy drink in silence. Then Tante Rita said, "Happy Saint Anne's Day! Happy birthday! I almost forgot to give you the day's felicitation. I will make it up to you later in the day. Now I must run. Pablita will be as cross with me as Nana is." Lala laughed. She knew Pablita. Pablita was Pita's older sister, who had gone to Washington with Tante Rita to take care of her needs. Pablita was even more strict with Doña Rita than Nana had ever been.

Lala did not argue with Nana this morning about which dress and slippers, sash and rebozo would be chosen for her to wear. That had been last year's

163

game, she thought. This year I am too old to play it.

Her mother and father came to give her birthday greetings. Suddenly the patio was filled with singing children.

> "*Ay, ay, ay, ay! Mira primero*
> *Donde pones los ojos, cielito lindo,*
> *No llores luego.*"

Lala went out on the *portal* to smile at them, clapping her hands in time with their singing.

"Señorita Lala, sing with us. Sing with us on your happy birthday morning," the children called to her.

Lala went to stand with them while she sang with them.

> "*Ay, ay, ay, ay! Canta y no llores,*
> *Porque cantando se alegran,*
> *Cielito lindo, los corazones.*"

Old Ramón the goldsmith and Old Pancho the cabinetmaker made their way through the throng of singing children. They were the oldest of all the hacienda men, so they were the chosen ones. Now they made a seat with their four hands to carry the small Patrona down the zaguán to all the patios and workrooms and houses of the people. The troubadour led the way, and the children followed, singing "Cielito Lindo," the children's song that is loved and sung from Taos to Mexico City. Everywhere they went, they were pelted by the grownups with colored egg shells filled with confetti.

> "*Ay, ay, ay, ay!*
> *Vienen bajando,*
> *Un par de ojetes negros, cielito lindo,*
> *De contrabando.*"

After breakfast, which was very merry, the family gave their birthday girl her gifts. Only the family gave her presents. For the hacienda children, this was their day, and on this day their little Patrona gave to them. It was her duty to see that on this day the children who would some day be her hacienda workers would be glad that she had been born.

Maman's gift was first. Old Ramón, who had made it, brought it, a high comb of tortoise shell and gold to hold her mantilla in place. Maman was thanked, and Old Ramón was praised. Then Tante Rita brought out her gifts. She had ordered them made in Washington, two corduroy riding habits: full, long-divided skirts, short, tight-fitting jackets, and matching hats with curling plumes. They had been made exactly

165

like the one she wore, even to the color, a dark, wine red. One was for Maman, and the other a birthday gift for Lala.

The man who worked in leather came next, bringing a carved sidesaddle, Tío Toto's gift. "But," Tío Toto said, "your aunt and I have another gift for you."

"Not now. Not now," Tante Rita hushed him.

Lala ran her fingers lightly over the saddle, looking at it, trying to hide the tears in her eyes. This was her first saddle. The one she used on the pinto was, like the pinto, for everyone to use. This was her saddle. It had been made especially for her. Finally she could thank both of them. How good they were to her. "Stay with us. We need you here."

"Washington needs them," her father said. Lala looked at her father. She had forgotten that this was the day he would give her the foal, if he was going to give it to her. She looked at him, one question in her sparkling eyes.

"Clop, clop, clop" sounded against the stones of the zaguán. "Clop, clop, clop." Chacho came first, a big smile for his little Patrona. Then came Luis, leading the foal.

The Patrón had prepared a little speech to say when he gave his only daughter ownership of her first horse. This was a proud day for him, an important day. But when the moment arrived, he found that his heart was too full to express what he felt. "For you, my little one," was all he could say. Lala also had thought that if the horse was given to her she could tell Papá how she felt. But now she said only, "Papá!" It was enough.

Lala walked up to the foal quietly. Even in her great delight, she must be careful not to startle it, not to frighten it. The foal nuzzled her. It knew her. "Little Beauty," Lala said softly, "I kiss you with my heart." These are the words that Spanish people say when they give their hearts away. She said them now.

The Patrón motioned for Luis to return the foal to the corral. "Papá." Lala found her voice. "Papá, Chacho is my groom boy. May he take the foal?" If Chacho had been knighted in the royal court of Spain, he could not have been more grateful.

Thoughtful like her mama, the Patrón thought, and the Patrona was thinking: Generous like her father. Thoughtful of people's feelings, generous in acknowledging them!

If Lala had known what her parents were thinking, she too would have felt knighted.

Late in the afternoon, the children's party was held

in the weaving room, and on the party table was every sweet bit known in hacienda cooking. Lala helped serve the children. This was her gift to them, that she, too, could serve.

At sundown, sitting in the patio before the workers came for evening prayer, Tío Toto said, "You have not asked what the other gift is that we have for you."

"I have so much," Lala said truthfully. "My heart is too full to hold even one more thing."

Tante Rita laughed. "It can hold this one." She nodded at her husband for him to tell the second gift. Tío Toto was pleased. He had wanted to be the one to tell her. "With your parents' permission, your aunt and I are taking you with us to Fort Union." Looking at the Patrón, he continued. "We will be gone three days only. Only three days."

Lala looked at her mother. Her mother nodded. She looked at her father. Please make him not say no, she prayed.

Her father said, "Your mama and I have discussed it. We will permit it for the short time you have promised." He looked at his brother, needing to hear again the promise of not more than three days.

"Will we go in the army ambulance with Outriders?" Lala asked, not daring to believe they would. She had not been to Fort Union. To go there, and with a military guard! She shook her head. It was difficult to believe.

"For all but the last ten miles," her uncle said. "Then your aunt wants us to ride into the fort. That is what she says. I do not know her reason. I seldom know her reasons."

Everyone laughed. Maman and Lala knew what Tante Rita's reasons were. The beautiful Doña Rita wanted to show her fine horse, her horsemanship, and her riding habit to the American ladies at the fort. Suddenly Maman knew why the riding habits had been the same color. What a picture they would make, the two French beauties riding in together. The thought pleased Maman. She was proud of both of them.

Much talk followed about what horses they would take, what people they would need. Finally all was decided. Pablita and Pita, of course. That was without question. Tío Toto would ride his albino; Luis would ride El Barb and lead Doña Rita's Arabian. Chacho would ride Casi and lead Maman's Arabian for Lala. It was decided.

The night passed. Lala had been afraid that morning might not come, but it came.

An hour after sunrise, they were on their way. The women rode in the ambulance. Tío Toto, Luis and

Chacho, and the horses they led rode with the Outriders. It was an impressive sight.

The Patrón and José rode with them a mile or so along the trail. As they passed the trading post, Canuto on his buckskin pony raised his hand in greeting.

"Look at his beaded jacket and buckskin leggings!" Tío Toto said. "Those are his royal robes. When he is working, he does not bother with buckskin clothing."

The Patrón shrugged. "I wonder what he wants now?"

"The Appaloosa foal," Luis said.

"That's one horse he cannot steal or buy or wangle as a gift," the Patrón said with conviction. They believed him. The foal was guarded well.

Inside the ambulance, Tante Rita said, "We will pass the immigrants somewhere on the trail. Poor dears, they must travel so slowly. We will stop," she promised. "You can see your Yellow Braids again."

Lala began to sing:

> "*I've come from Alabama,*
> *With my banjo on my knee.*
> *I'm going to Louisiana,*
> *My Susanna for to see.*

O, Susanna!
O, don't you cry for me."

As they rode on, Lala and Tante Rita spoke of the moment they would enter the fort of the United States government. Lala had ever before ridden her mother's Arabian. How her parents must trust her riding skill, she thought with pride. They would never let a horse be in unskilled hands. She had never ridden horseback beyond sight of the hacienda walls. She hummed a little made-up song:

> *"On a beautiful horse*
> *On a beautiful morning*
> *In the beautiful land of New Spain."*

"No," she corrected herself, "in the territory of New Mexico of the United States of America." It sounded wonderful to say, but it could not be sung, she decided. She looked at Chacho riding Casi beside her. He rides beautifully, but he would be embarrassed if I told him, she thought.

The rolling hills were lush with grama grass. The sky was all blue, with not even a tiny cloud to mar its blueness. The trail twisted around a rise leading down to the banks of the Río.

171

The cry to halt cut like a knife of steel through the morning stillness.

The Outriders, the riders, the plunging mules, and the careening carriage stopped on the edges of desolation. There was no time to turn aside. There was no time to look away. They had to gaze in horror at the scene of destruction before them.

"The immigrant train!" Tante Rita cried.

"What is left of it," her husband told her. "It is still smouldering."

"It must have happened less than an hour ago."

Lala could not cry out. She could not move or turn her eyes away. She had to look. She had to see the overturned, half-burned wagons and the people who had been in them. She had never seen death before. People had died in the hacienda, but death had come for them gently. She knew that when Indians were on the warpath, one band struck and ran and another band finished what had been started while the soldiers hunted for the first band. She had heard these things. She had not understood them. She thought in a daze: I must tell Pita that now I know why she was frightened when I went outside the hacienda wall.

Then she saw the doll she had given the little girl.

172

It was torn and partly burned and lay face down on the trail as if someone had placed it there carefully. She began to scream: "Where is Susanna? Find Susanna. Please somebody find Susanna."

"Annette." Tante Rita's voice cut through her screams. The horses had been brought forward. "Can you ride astride? Can you ride bareback? Good. Throw our saddles in the carriage, Chacho. Now ride."

"But the little girl, and Pita—where is Pita?"

"The little girl is not here, Annette, but our men will find her. Pita is safe in the ambulance. Ride. Ride fast."

Rita flicked the Arabian with her quirt, and Lala rode. Chacho rode beside her, matching his horse to hers.

Tante Rita turned to her husband. "You, of course, Miguel—" she used his name rather than the affectionate Toto, "will go on to the Fort. I expect it."

"Yes," Tío Toto told her. "I must go and you must send me. I will take two of the Outriders. The others will go with you. Soldiers from the fort will be sent out to bring the Indians to justice." He looked at his wife and she returned his look. This was not a time for endearments. Neither did they need them.

"Vaya con Diós, Miguel," she said.

"And you also," he replied.

And Doña Rita rode like a flurry of wind before a rain to overtake little Lala.

They tried to keep together—riders, Outriders, mule-drawn carriage—as they fled back to the safety of the hacienda. From there men would gallop out to track the Indians, to rescue the living if there were any, and to bury the dead.

At last they reached the trading post and the hacienda walls. Lala sat by the fountain. She sat quietly. She did not cry. She seemed not to listen when her mother tried to comfort her. Her father tried to reassure her: "They will find the little girl. All of my men that I can spare are helping the soldiers to track the Indians." She did not hear him. Chacho brought in the foal to show her that it was safe. She did not look at it or see it.

The hours of afternoon dragged by, turning the sunset sky from blue to gold to crimson. María came storming into the patio. "That Canuto is outside wanting to come inside. He has the little American with him. He says he has a message for the girl child of the Patrón."

"Bring them in," the Patrón told her.

They went out into the zaguán to meet him. María brought the sala chairs for the Patrona, Doña Rita, and the señorita Lala to sit on. They would sit, she thought furiously, not stand when that Indian came in!

Lala looked at her mother and her aunt. They sat as serenely as if seeing Canuto and the American child was an occurrence of every day. Please God, help me to be like them, Lala prayed.

Lala looked at her father. "Will he kill her?" she asked him.

"No. He may sell her to another tribe or keep her as a slave."

Freedom, Lala thought. That was one of the things the flag of the United States stood for.

Canuto came in, dragging the child, whose clothing was torn and bloodstained. Lala felt a hot surge of anger. Her mother touched her hand.

The Patrón spoke first. "You will be punished for this act, Canuto, by the Army of the United States."

Canuto answered with contempt: "They cannot punish me. The act was not mine. You saw me this morning when you passed the trading post. As many men as I have fingers on my hand saw that I stayed there all of the morning."

175

"Your men did what you told them to do."

"Who knows what my men have done, since none have been caught."

The Patrón spoke again. "Where did you get the child?"

"One of my braves found her." They knew he lied. The Indian turned away from the Patrón. "I will talk with the girl."

I will not ask him what he wants, Lala thought stubbornly. I will make him tell me. She sat there looking at the Indian, and now her look was as icy as his. The Patrón, even in his anger, had a moment of pride, looking at the two women and the girl. They sat so quietly, so fearlessly.

The silence was heavy, suffocating, a blanket of stillness. The hacienda women were not in sight, except for María, who sat by the door. Lala knew that close at hand were Nana, Pita, and Pablita. But there were no men. The men who were not tracking were guarding the horse herd. She continued to look at the Indian.

After an interval, Canuto spoke. "You own the Appaloosa foal. I want it." Lala did not answer. "This time," Canuto said, "I come not to buy it, not to steal it, not to hope for it as a gift or as a wager."

176

Lala made no answer, but she did not look away. She knew what he would say. She waited, an eternity it seemed, until he said it. "This time I come to trade. This," Canuto pushed the American child forward, "for the foal."

Lala's world spun. Now he had said it. It could never be left unsaid.

Her father said, "Little daughter, you do not need to do this. We will get the child." The Patrón in his grief spoke in Spanish, forgetting to hide his words in French.

Her mother, also in Spanish, said clearly, "Dear one, this you must decide. We cannot help you."

Lala looked at Tante Rita. Tante Rita was looking at her hands clasped in her lap. But as clearly as if she had spoken, Lala heard her words: "Every American has the right to have the opportunity to reach the full measure of his worth. Every American has the right to freedom—freedom from slavery, freedom from want, freedom from fear." Lala looked at the little girl, frightened, weary, bloodstained. The voice in her heart kept on. She could not stop it. "Every American has the responsibility to make those rights possible within his power."

Lala looked at Canuto. "I will trade, but on my

177

conditions. You must give us the little girl now. You cannot have the foal until it is old enough to leave its dam." She was surprised to hear her voice speaking so clearly, so calmly. At least he could not hear the sound of heartbreak.

Now that he had what he wanted, there was no need to hurry. Canuto took his time to answer. María could not contain her anger. She told him in Apache, "I see you have your pants on today." When he made no answer, she said in fury, "Do not pretend that you do not understand my language. An Indian understands an Indian." María could have been a buzzing fly for all Canuto cared.

He pushed the American child farther from him and spoke directly to Lala. "A voice that speaks without fear is to be trusted. I, Canuto, chief of my band, accept your word. The child now, the foal when it can leave its dam." He walked arrogantly to the door. María slammed it after him.

Lala turned to her mother, "Maman, will you accept an American daughter?"

"Annette, have I not told you that it is a small heart that has room for only one love?"

Lala felt comforted. Perhaps some day another horse . . . to fill the empty place in my heart . . . ?

She held out her hands to the little girl. "Come,

179

Susanna." The child did not move. She stood frozen with terror. Lala tried again. "Come, Susan. Come, Susanna." The little girl seemed not to hear her. Lala began to sing:

> *"I had a dream the other night*
> *When everything was still.*
> *I thought I saw Susanna*
> *A-coming down the hill."*

The little American came to life. With a sob she threw herself into Lala's outstretched arms.

Hours later, Papá and Maman walked into Lala's room, where two small girls were sleeping on a pallet on the floor.

"Says she will not sleep in her bed until Pancho makes one for her sister," Nana said fiercely. But, looking at her, Maman saw tears filling the wrinkles in her face.

"The new foal came an hour ago," the Patrón told Nana. "A perfect, honey-colored palomino. I want to waken the little one to give it to her."

Maman also spoke to Nana: "I tell him wait awhile. He must not cheat her of the experience of living with one's sacrifice or of the dignity of growing."

Nana answered: "Sí. Wait awhile before you give it."